# Asian Voices from Beantown

Short stories & poetry from the
Asian American Resource Workshop
Writers' Group

# DEDICATION

We welcome you to join us on a journey of wondrous memories, profound experiences, and forged truths. We hope you savor these stories because they were conceived with valiant heart, unabashed passion, and sweet agony. Enjoy!

-- The AARW Writers' Group

# CONTENTS

## *Resonant*

## *Persevering*

# ACKNOWLEDGMENTS

A special thank you to:

Saffron Circle
Asian Americans/Pacific Islanders in Philanthropy
Janet Gee
John Hsieh
Pauline Louie

## ABOUT THE ASIAN AMERICAN RESOURCE WORKSHOP

Founded in 1979 as one of the Boston area's first pan-Asian organizations, the Asian American Resource Workshop (AARW) is an intergenerational social justice nonprofit that promotes Asian American identity while addressing contemporary issues affecting our communities. To find out more, please visit http://aarw.org/

*Resonant*

# AMERICAN
By Yvonne Ng

"People would have a shit fit if I put together a White Writers' Group."

Mei Mei looked at Jerry and imagined his face dissolve into putridity. The beautiful brown eyes, double chin, hairy chest, man boobs, beer belly – all melting into soup, but his annoying insistence to press his point stopped the decomposition.

His tender lips kept talking, reminding her that she needed to react. Insult and walk away seemed like the best action because he was her boyfriend – at least until that conversation.

"You are so damn ignorant! I can't believe you just said something so stupid." Mei Mei screamed. Jerry responded, "I just don't agree with having a group like that. You set yourselves up to be a target… and you're separatists. I just don't get why you need a group like that in the first place."

"First of all, I'm a proud red blooded American. Second – until people stop saying to me – "oh you speak English really well.. or no, where are you REALLY from? when damn Charlestown isn't enough – that's when we wouldn't need groups like this. I've got to go." Mei Mei said as she turned to walk across the street. Her shoulders were rigid with anger and disappointment.

Jerry yelled, "That's it? You're gonna leave mad like that?"

Mei Mei said over her shoulder, "I'm not mad." She was sick from realizing that for the last four months they'd dated, she had no clue he was a want-to-be anti-racist racist. She wondered who the hell did he think he was dating anyway?

# THE HUDSON
## By Gay Eng

Henry Hudson
Was looking,
Searching for that secret passage.

I, too,
have been longing
for that elusive place.

I started in the middle of the Hudson,
went down to the New York Harbor,
Traveled upstate and downstate,
Journeyed to Hong Kong, Tokyo,
Beijing and Boston,
Searching for that meaning
far and near,
anything to grasp.

Back then,
the river
was always a barrier
difficult to cross,
cold and murky and wide.

We traveled up and down
along the water,
always on a Sunday.
My mama packed a lunch,
me and brother and sisters piled
into a beat-up gray Chevy,
on our one day off.

Forever on a journey,
my father
drove slowly.
Maybe he, too,
was searching for that passage.

# A BETTER LIFE
By Pong Louie

Sum Yiu Kwok was excited about finally getting his chance for a new and better life, in the United States. He felt that his opportunities in Hong Kong were limited. His brother, Kwong Yiu had already been in the US for a few years and finally sponsored him to come to the US. Although he was still in high school, he felt that it was his brother's duty to help him and it was about time he fulfilled this duty. He'd been dreaming about it since he was in Form 1, or seventh grade, as they call it the US.

It had been a long, boring flight, but it was now over. Sum Yiu tried to smooth his fuzzy hair down, took off his thick glasses and rubbed his eyes. He was no longer dreaming. The plane had landed and he was really here in the US. Excitedly, his tall, lanky body jumped up from his seat, almost hitting his head on the overhead bin. He tried to stretch, but everyone else was up and trying to collect their things and get off the plane too. He reminded himself that he had to be patient as he waited for his turn. He wasn't going to push and shove like people he'd seen from China.

As he waited for his baggage to come down and around, he saw Kwong Yiu. Sum Yiu was surprised. It'd been ages since they'd seen each other, but his brother didn't look very happy to see him and looked much shorter than he remembered. Sum Yiu hefted his bags off the belt, set them down and was ready to hug his brother.

"OK, let's go," Kwong Yiu said, turned around and started walking towards the exit.

Sum Yiu, struggling with his bags, tried to keep up with Kwong Yiu. "Ah Gaw! Can you help me with the bags?"

Kwong Yiu stopped, glared at his brother, yanked a bag from Sum Yiu's hand and took off again. Sum Yiu's heart sank. Why was his brother acting like this? He ran to keep up. Kwong Yiu threw the bags into the rust-orange colored Plymouth Valiant he'd borrowed, slammed the trunk lid shut and got in. Sum Yiu got in quickly.

"Ah Gaw, what's the matter? Why are you acting like this?"

"Don't complain. You wanted me to bring you here, so now you're here. I have a lot of school work to do and should be at work, but I'm here to pick you up. Be glad that I came. Let me make this clear now. You're here because YOU wanted to come. I got you here, but don't expect anything else from me. I can't afford the money or time to take care of you. You're on your own here, just like I've been for the past few years. I've arranged with a friend for you to stay with him and his roommate. The rent is only $70 a month for the three of you. You'll have to find a job to pay for it. I'll drop you off there, then I'm going to work. Al should be there. This is his car, so I'm leaving it there too."

Sum Yiu was in shock. He thought that he'd be living with his brother; that his brother would be helping him out, taking care of him. He didn't know what to say.

Kwong Yiu double parked in front of a four story, red brick town house, got out and ran into the building. He soon came back with another, somewhat older guy.

"This is Al; he's one of your roommates. He'll help you get settled. I'm going to work."

"But Ah Gaw…"

Kwong Yiu ignored him and left hurriedly.

"OK, Sum, Let's get your stuff upstairs and get you settled in." Al opened the trunk and took out the bags. He started taking one inside.

"Wait, what about the car? Don't you have to park it somewhere?"

"Just leave it there. Everyone in Boston double parks like that."

Al and Sum Yiu moved all his stuff up to the fourth floor walk-up apartment. Sum was exhausted and had already decided that he liked Al. He was much nicer to him than his own brother.

"So where's our other roommate? I'm anxious meet to him. Is he as nice as you or nasty like my brother was to me just now?"

"He's in New York visiting his mother. He'll be back tomorrow. He's a really easy-going guy, even nicer than me. Don't worry, you'll get along, even though he's a jook sing."

"A what?"

"A jook sing. You don't know that term? That's what we call American Born Chinese. I guess I've been here so long that I just assume everyone knows it."

"Why do you call them that?"

"That's just what they're called. That's what the old men who first came to the US called them. I guess it's because the old-timers thought they knew nothing, so their heads are hollow like the middle of a length of bamboo. People like me, who have been here a long time, are called jook kok, I guess they thought we know more and our heads aren't so empty, like the knots in the bamboo."

"So is his head hollow?"

"No, but we still call them all jook sing anyway. They're stuck with the name. So what do you feel like doing? You want to just get settled in and relax after your trip or you want to go somewhere?"

"Don't you have anything to do? Don't you have to work?"

"I work for the Boston Public Schools, so I have the summer off."

"Oh, you're a teacher?"

"No, I'm a liaison between the schools and the parents, but since the kids aren't in school now, I don't work either and I get paid during the summer. So if you want to go somewhere, I can take you. If you want to relax, I can leave you alone or we can sit and talk."

"I'm tired of sitting, I don't know about anywhere to go, so I'll go anywhere you want to take me."

"OK, let's start with Chinatown. If you want to walk, we can walk or I can drive."

"If it's not too far, let's walk. I want to stretch my legs a little."

"OK, let's walk; it's not far."

Sum looked around and asked, "Where's the bathroom?"

"Right down the hall on the left."

The floor creaked as Sum walked. He looked in the little bathroom. There was a toilet against the back wall with a tub on the right. The sink was next to the door. The tub had feet and a pipe sticking up from the far end with a circular tube attached to it, for the shower curtain. The floor was bumpy and the linoleum was a patchwork. The sink had water stains, a plug to stop water and two separate faucets, one for hot water and one for cold. Sum had second thoughts about what he'd gotten himself into. The whole apartment was rundown. But Al seemed nice and he had said that their other roommate was even nicer. And Ah Gaw had said that the rent was only $70 a month, that's just over $23 each, plus food. But what about utilities? He'd have to get a job, no matter how cheap it would be.

Al noticed the worried look on Sum's face as he came out of the bathroom.

"What's wrong? You'll be OK. Don't worry. Ping and I will get you through whatever comes up."

"I didn't know my brother would abandon me like this. I have to get a job so I can pay for this."

"Don't worry. I'll help you find one. In the meantime, I can cover your part of the expenses if needed. I make enough money and it doesn't cost that much to live here anyway."

"Thank you for everything. I don't know how I would survive without your help. I thought it would be my brother helping me. You don't even know me."

"I know your brother and I know you now. People have to help each other as needed. You'll be fine."

Al showed Sum how to get to Chinatown, up Shawmut Ave., across Berkeley St. and up Washington. It was easy. As they walked along Washington, Al explained how the Mass Pike was built through the community, separating Chinatown from the South End, where they lived. How they built the Southeast Expressway through Chinatown to the east, taking half the land and housing. Then they moved the "Combat Zone", Boston's red light district, to the area north of Chinatown and built the Theater District on the other side, effectively boxing Chinatown in and taking most of its land and leaving no room for expansion. He showed Sum New England Medical Center, always trying to take even more of Chinatown.

The tour of Chinatown didn't take very long. There wasn't much left, only about four blocks square. Sum noticed that there were a lot of restaurants and quite a few bakeries, gift shops and grocery stores. Food for the Chinese, junk gifts for the tourists, Sum thought, not much housing and no recreation, no parks.

"This is it? Nothing else? So small?

"No, there's not much else now." Al explained. "There is recreation though. You just can't tell. There's lots of gambling joints, but they're hidden, so they don't get raided. But that's the bulk of the recreation. That's why my friends and I do English classes and trips and stuff. The people need a lot more than gambling. Too many people lose their whole months pay in one sitting in those gambling joints."

"That's terrible. I didn't think it'd be so bad in the US. I'm tired; I need a nap. Can we go back now?"

The next day, Sum was still jet lagged, but feeling better. He went out to look around the neighborhood. When he got back to the apartment, Ping was back from New York and cooking dinner.

"Hi Ping, so you're my jook sing roommate."

"Yeah, that's me, the jook sing."

"Doesn't it bother you that people call you that?"

"Nah, that's what they call us. "

They talked and Ping seemed to be a nice guy. He was a little younger than Al and more Americanized, but not as much as Sum had expected. He also provided Sum the opportunity to practice English more.

Sum settled into his new life in Boston. Ping went to school, even during the summer. They and some other friends played basketball in the park behind their building every weekend.

Sum called Kwong Yiu, "Ah Gaw, we play basketball every weekend; you should come play with us some time."

"I told you; I don't have time to play with you. Don't bother me."

"I don't want anything from you. I just want to see you once in a while."

"No time, bye." Kwong Yiu hung up.

Sum found that he could ask his roommates anything anytime he needed to know something. They even gave him a hair cut when his hair got really long. On Saturday mornings, they taught English to older adults and that was where the trips Al had mentioned came from.

The trip to Montreal was tiring, but Sum had a lot of fun. They showed the "Saturday English Classes" students around Montreal and ate good food. The food was better in Montreal than in Boston. They toured Chinatown and did all the tourist things. Sum got to know some of the other volunteer teachers, most of whom were either immigrants or foreign students.

In September, he attended Newman Preparatory School as a senior. It was different from school in

Hong Kong, but not too hard to get used to, probably because it was a prep school, rather than a public school.

Al had found him a weekend job as a busboy in a Chinese restaurant. It was hard work and long hours, but the pay was more than enough for his expenses and pocket money. Overall, things were going well, but he missed his girlfriend back in Hong Kong something awful.

Sum had written her a few letters, but gotten no replies. He started singing "Wait a minute, wait a minute, Mr Postman…" around the apartment and people started calling him Postman. He decided to get up early one morning to call his girlfriend, when it was evening in Hong Kong. He cried and punched the wall. His fists hurt, but he didn't care. She didn't expect to ever have the chance to come to the US or to see Sum again. She'd found a new boyfriend. It was a unilateral decision, but it was over between them. Sum wanted to call his brother, but decided not to.

Al and Ping consoled him and did everything they could to help him get through it. It was tough and took time, but he got over her and went on with his new life. He applied to colleges and decided on engineering at Northeastern University. It seemed the best choice for him with its well-known Co-operative Education program. He could study half the year and work half the year and get work experience in his field of study. His first job wasn't what he'd expected. It wasn't an engineering job. He understood that after only a year, he wasn't ready to work as an engineer, but at a factory, on the assembly line? But it was a job and he made money, enough money that he decided to move to a nicer place with classmates, people his own age, instead of living with the great friends of his useless brother. He had new friends now, friends his own age.

Sum's job was boring and tedious. All day, he stood in front of a machine and stuck a metal plate into it to be stamped. He could do the job in his sleep. The end of the work quarter was near and Sum went to work as he did every day. He turned on his machine as he did every day. He picked up a sheet of steel to put into the machine to be stamped as he did every day. But the result wasn't the same as it had been every day of the quarter. The machine chomped on the steel plate faster than every other day. Sum's fingers were still in the machine and got chomped too. Sum blacked-out and woke up in the hospital with awful pain in his left hand. It was all wrapped up, so he couldn't see it.

The doctor explained to him what had happened. The machine stamped the tips of his fingers before he'd been able to get his hand out of the way. Apparently the company had sped up the machines without notifying the workers. The tips of all of the fingers on his left hand had been completely smashed. There was no way to save them. They had operated on his fingers, but Sum would need a few more operations and the recovery process would be long. He would have to wear a jig on his left hand to keep his fingers from curling up into uselessness. He'd have to have physical therapy after healing.

Sum wondered why he had wanted to come to the US so much. He wished he could go back in time to before he'd come to the US. He hadn't seen his brother since he first arrived.

His friends and former roommates came to visit

him, but not his brother.

"Al, does my brother know what happened?"

"Yeah, we told him, but he's been really busy. He'll try to come see you if he gets a chance."

"Yeah, right. I haven't seen him since he picked me up from the airport. I don't know why he hates me, but I think I'm dead to him."

He wondered how long it would actually take to recover and how much use he'll be able to regain in his left hand. He wondered if he'd ever be able to play the guitar again. He'd worked hard to learn to play it. It wasn't the greatest guitar, but it was his most valuable possession. It had been a graduation gift from his former roommates, the two guys who helped him so much when he was a FOB. He knew he'd never part with that guitar no matter what. The hell with his brother.

Sum called Kwong Yiu, "Ah Gaw, don't worry, I'll never call and bother you again. This is the last time. I just want to let you know that as far as I'm concerned, you're dead and no longer exist. Goodbye." He hung up and concentrated on his recovery.

# THE ANATOMY OF RED
By Alison Chan


She evokes bodily dreams
Of Blake's robin in a cage,
Poppy fields,

A ripe apple lush
With the promise
Of falling.

If only she knew
This journey towards love
I make,

The atoms of my blood
And the secret knowledge held in cells
Slowly unfolding

Our atavistic passions.

# HENRY JAMES
By Gay Eng

I used to think that people who watched TV were really dumb. But TV has gotten a lot smarter in the last few years. I have it on all the time now. When I go upstairs to fold the clothes, I flip it on. Then I go downstairs to start supper and I switch on the news. I like to watch Katie Couric while I'm eating. She's oddly comforting, like having a friend over for supper.

On dark, rainy days, I stay inside with TNT or Lifetime. I like action and love gone wrong. It keeps me occupied during those times when I don't know what to do, when I can't face the silence. Oh, don't get me wrong. I'm not one to feel sorry for myself. Sometimes I'll drive over to The Christmas Tree Shop and buy some knick-knacks for the hall. Or even call my friend in Florida.

It's hard sometimes being in a big, empty house. At least the kids are grown up and on their own. It doesn't really affect them. And there's no one to blame. I didn't lose everything. I still have this nice house in this nice town. I even go to church on Sundays and try to believe in God.

After he was laid off, Henry didn't say much. He would go down to the basement and exercise. For the first month, he got a lot of calls from job agencies and phone interviews. But he was never called back. I got a job at the new LL Bean store and we had enough to live on for the time being. We even went out to eat once a week. Henry started talking about opening his own company as a financial adviser. He could help people with bankruptcies, foreclosures and taxes. He started looking at real estate in town and was considering renting a storefront on Rt. 9.

Then Henry started selling things. He sold his Nautilus and treadmill. I didn't mind. I never used those hulking machines anyway. I liked to go outside for exercise, and didn't understand spending hours sweating in a basement. Maybe I should have known when he sold his beloved iPhone and laptop. But he just said he wanted to simplify and didn't need fancy gadgets. After all, we still had three other computers.

When I heard about the Lehman Brothers support group, I urged Henry to go. He went to one meeting, said it was full of young fools, and never went back. Then it was spring and I was glad to be outside with the fresh-cut grass, the blooming forsythia and the fragrant lilacs. Henry cut back some brush and even planted a few new trees. Spring was a time of new beginnings. We talked of buying land in the western part of the state and raising sheep. Henry had actually grown up on a sheep farm in Wyoming before going to Dartmouth. I will always remember the first time I saw him. He was so different from the awkward boys who usually came to campus from MIT. I first heard his loud laughter outside my open window. I looked outside from the second story and saw him with two other guys—all looking up with eager smiles.

"Hey!" he shouted. "We're looking for some Wellesley girls."

"Whom are you looking for?" I asked.

"Well, no one in particular. Are you busy tonight?"

Blushing, I said, "No, I'm working on a paper."

"You have no business working on a Saturday night. Come on down and bring two of your friends."

And that was how I became acquainted with the easy-going and highly-intelligent Henry James Suzuki. Henry was third generation Japanese-American. His father started the sheep farm after being released from the internment camps after the War. His mother spun the wool and knitted garments that she sold to the stores in town. Being Chinese, my mother was wary of a Japanese boyfriend, but Henry won her over and charmed her just like he charmed everyone else that came his way. After I graduated with my English degree from Wellesley, we married and moved to Philadelphia, where Henry finished his business degree from Wharton. Then it was on to Wall Street and the directorship of the Boston office.

We lived a charmed life, raised two beautiful girls with Ivy League educations. We had lively supper parties with stimulating conversations. I was in the garden club and volunteered for the historical society.

Then, suddenly, it was over, in The Collapse. I thought Henry took it well. After all, our house was paid for and the girls were working. We lost most of our retirement savings, but we had time to make it up. He talked more and more of the sheep. The worst thing was the smell and the clean-up, he said. After college, he had vowed never to go back to the farm. We only went once right after we got married. Having grown up in the tenements of New York, I was amazed by the wide open spaces and a bit frightened of the animals. I did get on a horse and rode a few times but that was it. I wasn't roaming with the sheep and dogs. Soon after that, his parents sold the farm and retired to Seattle.

Henry was considerate to the end. He didn't do it in the house. He went out into the woods on the other side of town with his hunting rifle. He left a note in the car.

# NOBODY HAS A LEG LIKE I DO
## by Amanda Chiang

I have a bump in my knee.

It isn't a big bruise or a wart. It's an unusual bump and it hurts. A lot.

The bump quickly turns into a lump, and swells up real fast. The doctor does all sorts of tests on me, like x-rays and a CT scan.

The doctor says I have cancer.

Cancer is something that kills your good cells, and it can grow and spread to other parts of your body. If it is not treated it will take your life.

The cancer I have is called osteosarcoma. It is spreading rapidly, and the only way to stop it is to remove the part of my leg below the knee. Amputation, they call it.

No . . . no no no. I look at mom and dad. I want my leg. Please . . . don't let them take away my leg.

Mom and dad squeeze my hands and hug me to give me strength, but that is all they can do.

Lying in the hospital bed, I wonder what it will be like without half my leg: no more running or playing ball. Only right-footed shoes and socks. I will have only five toes. Will I be able to pump myself on the swing with one leg? How will I climb on the jungle gym at school?

I am rolled into the operation room.

Goodbye toes. Goodbye leg.

~    ~    ~

The surgery is over. I can't look down at that empty space, at the stump that will be with me forever. I stare at the ceiling, forcing my eyes away from the bandage.

Mom and dad, my cousins, friends, classmates, and teachers have filled my room with balloons, stuffed animals, toys, and cards. But none of these could fill that empty space below the bandage.

On the fifth day, I gather up all my courage— and look at it. I cry. My leg isn't there anymore! I will never be able to walk or run or kick balls like the other kids. I will never look normal again. I bury my head under my pillow and never want to come out.

Mom and dad try to talk to and encourage me, but I don't feel like talking. Friends come, but I don't want them to see me.

One day the doctor asks me if I want a new leg. A new leg? It would be artificial, which means it's not real. It would be made of metal with a plastic foot. She says I would be able to run and walk and kick balls in no time.

I practice and practice and practice with the new leg. It is very uncomfortable at first. I can't feel the floor, and the leg doesn't listen to me at all. I get mad at it when it is naughty and doesn't go where I want it to, but when it is good I put a sticker on it.

There were no stickers when I started with two crutches.

There were a few when I practiced with one.

Now that I don't need crutches, my leg is covered with stickers. As time goes by, my fake leg feels more and more real. I am walking without hobbling, and soon I am going to try skipping. I'm sure I will be able to climb the jungle gym again like I used to.

My friends at school think it's cool. Nobody else looks like me, and nobody has a leg like I do.

Hello, leg...

# POETRY AFTER A SHIJO READING
## By Gay Eng


E-commerce

E-commerce
can take me
places
I couldn't ever
Imagine before.

What happened
to my life,
my determination?

I glance
down
And so many years
have floated away.
Memories just
like yesterday are
driving by in the fast lane.

The snow,
the cold,
Baby, it just seems
like tomorrow
comes and goes.

It, too
will pass.

The snow

The snow stopped
our first
arranged meeting
two weeks ago.
Next the ice
storm in all its fury
prevented our face to face.
It's preordained,
you texted.
We shall never meet
In person,
just be friends
on FB.
We should be
content with all that,
not push it any further.

But what
if you are the one?
I thought silently.
I can't let fate
Intervene.
Sometimes
action is required.

# MISSING YOU
By Yvonne Ng

You used to tell me everything… ok… not really. You'd generally tell me all the bad stuff. The hurt, sorrow, loneliness used to fill me up. But the thing that made you come to me most was the anger.

I think it's because you grew up so Catholic and Chinese. Damned if you sinned and damned more so if you ever disobeyed mom and pop.

You hardly ever had that 'American' type of brutal anger sessions, expressed in lots of shouting and throwing things about.

You never even knew how to fight back. Remember that Black kid in second grade who was ready to kick your ass because you told on him to the teacher? You were so scared when he got to you after school and kicked your back pack. You really should have listened to your sister, when she told you to fight back. That would have been an interesting thing to hear about. But then again – what did you know about all that?

You learned about aggression the passive way. It can be insidious and even effective, but only some of the time… not all the time.

And when you came to me and told me all the things that made you upset, you never really forgot or forgave.

Tough to be a good Catholic, huh?

But these days, you haven't come to me. I miss you even though I see you all the time. It's because you don't reveal much to me. You keep it all in your head.

That's not good you know. The crappy stuff will plant itself and fester and you know what that build up of stress can lead to? Yup a relapse.

Ok. They'll never admit to it but your emotions make you real, so why the heck wouldn't your body respond to the stress overload? I can see your tension making your eye twitch.

I'm only saying all of this because you forget that I'm here to help. So you should let me. I mean, you always feel better after you talk to me. Just come back, ok?

# GIFT
By Cynthia Yee

My family did not believe in buying gifts for birthdays and Christmas. They always gave me red envelope money for the Chinese Lunar New Year and my birthday with good wishes and something about saving the money for the future or letting it grow baby coins in the bank. Every year my cousin, Albert, could pick one toy for a Christmas present and I was invited to go along. I just helped Albert decide: a train, a toy gun, or a cowboy outfit. I would just look in the shiny cases at the Jordan Marsh Department Store wishing. Our parents had mutually agreed that they would keep it simple "lo lo sit sit" and not buy gifts for each others' children requiring a return gift, a polite way of repayment. It was considered an unnecessary frivolity in our frugal immigrant life.

My tall and handsome Uncle Eddie had a wife and six children in China and was a waiter at the Cathay House on Beach Street. He lived alone in Chinatown but he came for dinner on the men's "day-off-foo" and holidays. One day he brought me a Gift. The gift was two books. One was called "The Sun" and the other, "A Book of Natural History." I was amazed and thrilled to receive a Gift. I had never owned a book and aside from the Maryknoll nuns seldom received a gift. I would pore over those two books every chance I had. Aside from my treasured Comics collection, they were the only two books I owned. The illustrations of the fiery sun with its black sunspots and its planets and the beautiful pictures of great varieties of plants and animals mesmerized me;

their categories and their evolutionary history intrigued me.

For my High School graduation, my sojourner Uncle, gave me an expensive Omega watch by which I checked my time all the way through College. When the time came, he encouraged me to go to a good Graduate School. I have always kept that Omega watch. When I look at it, I think of him and his respect for me.

When I was twenty-four years old, adventurous, well traveled I thought , and naiive and before China opened to tourism, I decided to go to China. He asked to come along. We traveled together to China with visas from Canada. He wanted to see his wife and grown family. I was just curious to see the land of my parents' birth. He had not seen his wife and children in over twenty-five years and never met his grandchildren. As the train chugged into Kwangchow from Hong Kong, we conversed and admired the verdant green rice paddies and he talked to me about his younger days in China. This was a time of return and reunion for my sojourner uncle and for me, his American born niece, entrance into an unknown way of life. For five weeks he had family dinners and conversation and rejoiced in the warm company of his large and loving family. Just five weeks out of a lifetime.

Years later, back in the United States and our American lives, I helped to negotiate with two alienated governments, China and the United States, to bring his wife and two of his sons, their wives and their daughters to America. But he died before their arrival. Our trip would be the last time he would see his much yearned for family. His two young granddaughters grew up to become accomplished students and professionals and told me recently of a return trip to the new China for a family reunion. They honored the sacrifices of their deceased grandparents and toasted to their memory.

I have now, in the many years that have passed, lost The Sun book but have kept "The Book of Natural History" with its dog-eared pages and torn and frayed cover and binding. I keep it at my Cape Cod house where I planted a large garden. I experimented with a variety of seeds, mulches and soil mixtures augmented with truckloads of manure and topsoil. I became a teacher of science to young children. Planting seeds and Spring bulbs, studying the patterns of the night sky, the Earth, the Sun, the Moon and the Stars I felt like a traveler in the immense Universe. Gardening and cooking, teaching and experimentation, and studying science phenomenon continue to give me great personal joy.

My Uncle Eddie's granddaughter, Megan, tells me how lucky they feel to be living in the United States, with its many opportunities. I pause and think how very lucky I am for her Grandfather, my tall and handsome Uncle Eddie who I called Ai-Sook, Eldest Young Uncle, who gave me the gift of two books, for the possibilities he saw in me before I saw them in myself.

For the dreams I helped to make come true for him and his family, I hope it was a good enough repayment for a more than good enough Gift.

*Written in loving memory of Moon-Fun Yee, my dear Uncle Eddie who I called Ai Sook.*

*Persevering*

# FIGHT FOR RIGHTS
By Pong Louie


"Any luck today?" Lan asked.

"No, it's the same everywhere. I can't stand it anymore," Minh answer.

"Well, you have to do something about it. You can't just keep working at that restaurant and not get paid for your work. It's not fair."

"What can I do? There's nothing I can do about it."

"You can talk to your co-workers first. Get them to all work together against Li."

"They're all in the same situation. They don't know what to do either. It's useless."

"If you don't talk to them, how do you know that they don't know anything? Talk to them tomorrow; promise me."

"OK, I'll talk to them but it won't do any good. I'm too tired for this; I'm going to bed. It's work, sleep, work, sleep, every day, six days a week."

Still tired the next morning, Minh got ready for another eleven hour day at the restaurant . He was reluctant to talk to his co-workers, but he knew that his wife was right. They had to do something about the situation. They had to get paid for all their work hours and Li shouldn't be taking their tips. But Li had gone to law school; shouldn't he know and follow the law?

Minh looked for opportunities to talk to his co-workers, picking the ones he thought would more willingly agree, to talk to first. It turned out to be surprisingly easy. They were mostly fed up too. But what would the next step be? Some had suggested that they go to the Chinatown People's Progressive Association for help. That's what they had heard people on the streets say, but he was hesitant to go to them. People also said that they're commies. He hated the commies who had ruined Vietnam, splitting it into north and south. But he also knew that Lan, being from China, would support the idea.

So they went to CPPA for help. The people there got all the information from all the workers. They took the case to the Attorney General. It took months for things to happen, but they were finally getting somewhere. They would get back pay and tips paid out to them. Li was forbidden to fire them for reporting him. He had to change his practices and be monitored.

Minh was still tired and he regretted not having studied harder in high school and that he never joined his friends at CPPA for ping-pong when they went. He had to admit it when he saw a couple of his former teachers at CPPA. At least he'll be paid better from now on.

"OK, it's almost over now. Things should be better soon," Minh told Lan.

"Yes, it was the right thing to do. Now all of us can have a somewhat better life, not just you and me and the kids, but all the other workers and their families too."

The doorbell rang and Lan got up.

"No, it's late, I'll get it." Minh went downstairs to see who it could be.

Lan heard three loud bangs. They sounded like gunshots, so she ran down the stairs and saw Minh lying in the doorway in a pool of blood and screamed.

New England Medical Center was just across the street, but it was too late. Minh's body was lifeless. All three shots were to his head. Lan held Minh in her arms, crying.

# CHANGE
By Gay Eng


The rules were changing. The money was dwindling. Who was there to go to anymore and where was there to turn? Even a glimmer of light, a glimpse of hope could help these people on their way. But there was no end in sight. The line was getting longer and the days were getting colder. Bread and cheese. That was all there was today and who knew if there was enough for everyone? People were coming out now with only half blocks of cheese and one loaf instead of two loaves of bread.

Laura wished she didn't have to be in this line and wished her Mom would come home today. Just then she saw another girl from the sixth grade. But the girl turned away quickly and ignored her. Laura bit her lip to keep from crying. Dad and her brother, Petey, were scouring the city, picking up cans.

Mom had gone back home to look for a job, she said. But California was even worse than here. Laura couldn't believe she had abandoned them. One night last month, she had heard her parents shouting in their bedroom. Loud, angry voices came through the wall, but she couldn't catch the exact words. The next morning while Laura was eating her Cheerios, Mom hugged her and told her to be good. Then she was nowhere to be seen after school.

That evening, Dad told her to cook some spaghetti and didn't answer her questions about Mom. He drank a whole six pack and wouldn't talk at supper or for the rest of the evening. Mom called her every week but it wasn't the same as being there. Laura didn't have much to say. Sixth grade was a bore, and her favorite class, Art, had been cut.

She pretended everything was normal at school and only told her best friend, Jessie, about her Mom. She missed Mom's chicken salad sandwiches and fruit salad at lunch, and hated the school lunches. Petey didn't seem to mind and sometimes stopped by her table to eat her leftovers.

At supper, Dad would often say he wasn't hungry and Petey ate his share, too. He would often say he had eaten a big lunch at the church where he did odd jobs for food.

As Petey grew taller, Dad grew thinner, and Laura was starting to get breasts. Then the bleeding started and Laura cried herself to sleep every night.

# BABA
By Cynthia Yee

Walter (Baba) and May-Soon Gee Yee,
reunited in
Boston, Massachusetts, 1948

In the hills of Hoisan near the South China Sea
lived a six year old girl named Kwan Hoong. She was
the youngest daughter in a family of three daughters.
Theirs was a disfavored family because in her village,
sons were prized above all else. She sat on top of her
hilltop village looking as far as she could see,
wondering how big the world was, wondering how far
away the Land of the Flowery Flag was, how long it
would take to sail there, and how long it would take
for her to find her Baba and he her. "Perhaps he has
already forgotten me," she whispers to herself.

"When I was born he was already away. And now the Japanese are coming to kill us. We must hide in the village and smear soot on our faces so they cannot see how we look." Her mother used to live in the city of Kwangchow. Kwan Hoong's mother detested the country village life but had to come here to hide when the warning came that the Japanese were coming. There were fierce soldiers killing and hurting people and stealing their food, it was said. Now she is already six years old. Her mother only took one pot with her from their city home because she was sure she would not stay more than one year. Now here it is six years later and they are still here. Her father is a soldier in the Land of the Flowery Flag fighting the enemy in another land so her mother had not received any letters or money from him in seven years. She heard her mother cry at night when she thought Hoong was sleeping.

Kwan Hoong liked to watch her mother and her eldest sister, Lin, sew at night. Every night they took the fancy silk clothes her auntie had given them from her dead auntie's wedding chest. Kwan Hoong liked to feel the shiny silk and the colorful embroidery. Mother and Lin would re-cut and re-sew them until they looked new. Every morning they would go out to sell the re-made clothes.

Her dead auntie had been sad one day. Her husband had been away in the Land of the Flowery Flag for seven years too. She sent her little son out to play with Hoong's father when her father was a little boy. While her son played, she hung herself. Then later her little son got sick and died too. Now her new auntie helped her mother by giving her the dead auntie's clothes to remake to sell. Her mother and Lin also carried bags of rice from one village to another to sell. Lin was twelve and carried the bag of rice on her back. Her mother told her to just walk slowly if it felt too heavy.

They were always busy. Sometimes they dug for wild yams and taro and sometimes they only had wild grasses for their food. And sometimes they just went to bed hungry. Mother always gave her and her eight-year-old sister the little food they had. Her mother walked one full day to the Hoisan seashore to buy the salty brine the salted fish was soaked in with the money from the clothes and the rice. It gave some flavor to their rice gruel.

Kwan Hoong would ache with hunger at night and she would dream about the day her Baba from the Land of the Flowery Flag would come home from the War, how he would hold her up high and twirl her and give her sweet candy to eat. And love her like a Father would surely love his daughter.

*Dedicated to the memory of my third sister, Kwan Hoong, who died in infancy in 1930's wartime China and also our Baba, Walter Yee, who served as a U.S.A. Army Corporal in WWII Germany and France. He was separated from our mother, May Soon Gee Yee, for 15 years. Kwan-Hoong and her Baba never met because of the corrosive effects of the U.S. Chinese Exclusion Act. The U.S. government in 2012 issued an apology for the discriminatory Chinese Exclusion Act. Thank you to my eldest sister, Yerk Lin Yee aka. Gum Tong Yee, for sharing the stories of her life in WWII China.*

# OPEN PALMS
By Yvonne Ng


What is it inside us that is
willing to risk
exposure?

Vulnerably opening our palms
hefting the weight of our beating hearts,
giving them to others as
offerings.

Others who also have perfectly
good and sturdy hands and
throbbing tickers.

But their hearts
are comfortably ensconced
in ribs, and skin.

And their hands
can be
clenched.

# CYCLIST 44
By Pong Louie

Don Che Wong was pumped. This was his seventh bike-a-thon. Seven years ago, he'd only been able to find a dozen people to ride in his first bike-a-thon fundraiser. Now, starting to bald and ten pounds heavier, for his seventh one, it had grown to 90 people. He'd always known that it would never grow to be like the March of Dimes' Walk for Hunger, but even 90 was huge for him. People came from everywhere, high schools, colleges, banks, community organizations, friends, friends of friends, everywhere. Don was so excited.

Don finished checking bikes, woofed down a roast pork bun, stood up on a bench and cupped his hands around his mouth.

He shouted, "Is everyone ready?!"

A few people looked up at him.

"Is everyone ready?!" he shouted again with his arms raise in the air.

Some people got the idea and shouted back, "Ready!"

Don repeated his action, "I can't hear you! Is everyone ready?!"

This brought a big, loud response, "READY!"

Definitely not Boy Scout camp, Don decided and reminded people to have water with them and made sure they knew who the guides were. He pointed out the way and introduced a tall, buff young man as Larry, the lead guide.

"OK, let's go!" Larry shouted and took off. People followed him. Don fell-in in the middle of the crowd.

Lam, the short, stocky guy, would be the tail. They rode up to the corner and took a right onto Summer Street past the huge post office at South Station, over the bridge and a left towards Boston Harbor along East First Street. It was their first time using this route. It was very scenic along the water with a couple of beaches along the way.

After the first beach, they stopped at the first checkpoint. Don, Larry and Lam made sure everyone had enough water and offered granola bars to anyone who was hungry. They made sure there were no bike problems and continued.

As they approached the second beach, Don saw a petite teenage girl swerve into a tree up ahead and fall.

"Are you OK?" Don asked as he rushed up to her. She was one of the Charlestown High students.

Mei Ming Chan showed Don her scraped arm, speaking to him in Cantonese. "Ngo jiek sau shoon joh."

"Shoon joh, don hai ng hai ho tung jeh, hai ma?" Don asked as he took out the first aid kit from his bag. He wanted to make sure it was just scraped and not broken.

"Ng hai ho tung. Mo toon." Mei Ming assured Don that it wasn't broken.

He bandaged the scrape and they were on their way again. He knew it had to happen. Someone had gotten hurt every other year, so why not this year too, especially with so many people riding. But they weren't on their way again. Mei Ming had a flat. So that's why she hit the tree!, Don thought as he grabbed the tire repair kit and tire irons from his saddle bag. He was glad that the wheels and brakes were quick release.

All the other riders had passed and Lam came up. "You need help?"

"Nah, it's just the front, easy enough. You keep going and we'll catch up." Don released the brake shoes, then the wheel. He patched the tube and put everything back together. "OK, all set."

Mei Ming apologized, "I'm sorry I broke your bike."

"It's not my bike. We borrowed it from the city. I'm sorry it broke and you got hurt."

"Will the city be angry because I broke it?"

"No, they understand that the bikes will get flats and now, they won't even know that it had a flat."

"Thank you." Mei Ming took off quickly to try to catch up with the rest of the riders.

Before Don knew it, they were all at the turn around point. It had been a quick, easy ride with a nice breeze off the harbor.

Lam stayed in the middle on the way back, so Don took the tail.

At the turn off the bike path back onto the street, Don hoped that everyone knew to turn and didn't go straight and around to Castle Island. He hung around a few minutes to see if anyone came back around. No one did, so he continued on.

Just before the bridge, Don saw Lam off to the side on a grassy area under a big tree. "What happened? Or are you just resting in the shade?"

"A screw came loose and fell off. This fender support got caught in the spokes and Mindy fell," Lam explained as Mindy showed Don her bandaged knee.

"I'm gonna take the fender off because we don't have the screw or anything that can replace it to reattach the support."

Don examined the fender support, "Shoulda brought some electrical ties, but never thought I'd need them. Now I know better for next year. Hope the city doesn't get pissed that we took it off... But Jessica's really nice, she should understand." He stuck the fender into his pannier and put some of the bottles of water on top, to keep it from bouncing out of the bag and they all took off again.

A few minutes later, they were back at the Gateway Park and found everyone had stopped to wait for them. The guides took a head count to make sure everyone was there.

"So Nam, what'd you get?"

"89, what about you, Larry?"

"I got 89 too. How 'bout you, Don?"

"Same, we're missing someone." He couldn't believe it. They'd never lost anyone before. He wondered if all three of them could have counted wrong and come up with the same number.

Don climbed up on a bench again. He stuck his thumb and index finger into his mouth and whistled loudly, ignoring the disgusting taste of the grease and dirt that had accumulated on them. It was no time to worry about that. They had to find the missing person. He shouted, "Everyone look around and see if any of your friends is missing."

A few whispers went around the crowd, "Someone's missing?"

"Where's Sut Chung? I don't see her; she's number 44," another teen said, then shouted, "Sut Chung, are you here?"

There was no response.

Don repeated the teen's shout. "Sut Chung, are

you here?"

Again, there was no response.

"OK, everyone continue to Boston Common for the picnic." Don shouted, then jumped off the bench to talk to the chubby teen who had identified the missing person.

"What's your name?"

"Choon Joi," she replied as she pushed her long fine hair out of her face.

"OK, Choon Joi, do you mind coming with me to look for Sut Chung? I don't know what she looks like. Describe her to me."

"Sure, she's my little sister. She looks a lot like me, but not so fat. We don't always get along, but she's still my sister and I have to find her. My mother will kill me if I go home without her. She'll think I lost her on purpose. I promised I'd look after her."

"I can take over as one of the guides if you want," Steve volunteered.

"Great, Steve, thanks. You take the middle and I'll go back to being the tail," Lam said and motioned for Larry to go.

Don looked at Choon Joi's worried face and said, "Don't worry, we'll find her," trying to sound confident. "Are you and your sister Charlestown High students too?" Don wanted to calm himself down as much as trying to calm Choon Joi down.

"Yes, she is ninth grade; I am eleventh grade."

The two of them started making their way back along the way they had come. Don led the way, looking around for a Chinese girl on a bike. He looked back every couple of minutes to make sure he didn't lose Choon Joi too. He couldn't imagine trying to explain to their parents how he'd lost both sisters.

As they rode along, Don decided that the most likely place for someone to get lost would be at the turn-off near Castle Island. When they got back there, they stopped and looked around carefully, but didn't see Sut Chung.

Don decided, "OK, you go that way around toward Castle Island. I'll go around this way and see if we see her. If not, we'll have to go back along the beach again."

"OK," Choon Joi answered and started out counter-clockwise while Don went clockwise.

Don stopped suddenly and called out to Choon Joi, "Wait, is your sister riding a white city bike too?"

"Yes."

They rode slowly around the circle towards Castle Island, looking for Sut Chung. There were other white bikes and there were other Chinese people, but not Sut Chung.

About two-thirds of the way around, Don saw Choon Joi coming toward him from the other direction, alone. Where the heck is she? He asked himself. We have to find her.

They reached each other with questioning faces, hoping there was more to report than just not finding Sut Chung.

Choon Joi shouted at the top of her lungs, "Sut Chung! Where are you?"

Don saw someone sitting on the grass near a white bike in the middle of the circle. She raised her head out of her hands. She looked like she had been crying. Relief replaced fear on her face. She jumped up and ran toward Choon Joi, ready to hug her.

But instead of hugging her sister, Choon Joi started scolding her.

"What's the matter with you? Why are you just sitting here? You scared us."

"Choon Joi, stop! Don't yell at her. It's not her fault." Don could see that Choon Joi didn't like being stopped and wanted to continue. He gave her a look that stopped her and he patted Sut Chung on the back and told her, "It's OK, we've found you now. We won't lose you again. You must be hungry. Let's get to the Common."

Don took his cell phone out and called Larry. "We found her and we're coming now. Let people know."

Don led the way with Sut Chung in the middle. He kept looking back along this last mile of the ride.

# OWL
By Amanda Chiang

Perhaps I had loving parents. Perhaps I had brothers and sisters. I will never know. It is the owl who has been with me, watched over me, since the beginning of my memories.

In my five-year-old mind, I could vaguely see the smoke, the red-orange brightness dimmed with dark ashes; could vaguely hear the screams, the wails, the savage grunts and yelling. I can still feel the burning in my eyes, nose, and throat, that awful feeling of being on the brink of suffocating, as someone held me tight to their chest. I can still feel the thumping of that someone's heart beating wildly against my own.

I must have passed out then, for I next saw a furry face with great brown eyes staring down at me, and intense yet curious look that demanded me to obey but also made me feel safe. I struggled to sit up beneath the stiff, heavy arm that lay across my stomach, the arm that did all it could to protect me. Those round eyes never wavered as they watched me stand up: the owl stood as tall as me.

We gazed at each other for a long while. Occasionally it would blink, its eyelids slowly sliding down to cover its clear blue eyes, then slide back up. Those blue eyes, and its feathers that were a shade brighter than the cleanest snow, stood out brilliantly against our lifeless surroundings.

It turned around, slightly fluffing its feathers. With a great beat of its wings it took flight, soaring upwards in a slant oval and back, hovering a few feet above me. I knew what it wanted.

She led me through the charring remains of houses that once stood proud and bloody bodies that were once lovingly familiar. I tried not to look and focus on her white wings, but something in the nature of the revolting and grotesque attracted me, and I peeped, again and again. Sometimes I would trip, horrified to find myself on a headless torso, a squishy organ, or just a leg that lay by itself in the soot. The owl would turn back and hover close to me, then fly ahead again once I stood.

By the time we reached the outskirts of the village, evening had set. It was my first dose of the outside world, and I never knew how far and wide green grass could grow. My legs were shaking dangerously, and I collapsed. I rolled around and inhaled the sweet-smelling grass deliciously. The owl landed beside me, standing still and watching me. Soon though, she nudged me with her wing. I sighed and reluctantly pulled myself up, trudging after her on feet that no longer wanted to defy gravity.

At the river, the owl watched me clean my grubby and filthy self, washing away the soot, dirt and blood that covered me from head to toe. I lay on the bank for a short nap, and when I awoke I found a small pile of fruits and nuts. The sight of them brought pangs to my stomach, and I devoured them all eagerly. For dessert, the owl brought some little red flowers, and I sucked their nectar blissfully. Night soon came. The owl pointed to a huge tree nearby, where we will spend the night, I snuggled inside the tree trunk and she well-hidden on one of the high branches.

In the morning we shared another pile of fruits and nuts she had gathered, and went on our way. It was then I wish I knew how to speak owl, or she how to speak my tongue, for I longed to know where we were going.

After another day's walk, we arrived at a small temple. I walked up the steps to the gate, and the owl descended, standing with me. She pecked at the door with her beak, and I gave a few knocks to help. A nun opened the doors and took me in with great kindness.

As I followed her, I looked back to see the owl still standing at the gate. I beckoned her to come, but she gave a nod of her head, and flew off.

My heart sank, but I was relieved when she came to visit me in the evening, and the next morning, and every day afterwards.

The nuns gave me good food and clothed me warmly, and I would sweep the floors and dust the deity statues to pass the days. Sometimes I would play in the courtyard while they chanted in low, humming tunes, songs I did not recognize but they said they would teach me if I wanted to learn.

The owl's daily visits have become weekly.

Aside from my daily chores, the nuns have started teaching me characters, starting with numbers. I want to strike the huge bell too—it gives out such a satisfying loud and low "bong" that seems to echo for miles and miles, but the nuns say I will have to wait until

I am older and stronger.

She now visits me once a month, the first day of each month for five months now. Her next visit is a day away, and I can't wait to read to her the new passage I learned in the beginner's scroll. Each time she brings me the little red flowers to suck on, and I would tell her stories about the nuns and what I've been studying. She would cock her head while listening, and trill when she's pleased.

This time she brought a huge bouquet of little red flowers, and spent an extra two hours with me. I knew the time had come. She dug her beak into her right wing, plucking out a gleaming, snowy feather. She came close and stuck it behind my ear, paused to look at me, and turned around. With a flap of her wings she took off, soaring into the purple-pink rays of dusk. I scrambled to the bell tower, struck it three times with all my might, and watched her white silhouette until it became a dot. The feather caressed my cheek softly as the low bong hummed through my body, and through the evening air.

# LEDGE
By Yvonne Ng


Connie exhaled. She needed to move five inches to her left and let gravity hurl her 80 feet to the sidewalk. Just as she shifted an inch closer, she caught movement through a window of a bare bedroom across the street.

She saw that little brown girl pirouette. A pink restaurant napkin with the ends cut into strips surrounded her waist from wide blue suspenders. As the girl twirled, the makeshift tutu would whirl. Although the girl was quite petite, her white t-shirt was much too small for her. The girl jumped and her plié was amazingly graceful.

Connie was transfixed by her performance. The girl lifted her skinny arms into an arc above her head when she noticed Connie outside. Slowly the girl put her arms down and walked to the window. She hefted the heavy window pane wide enough to shove her face sideways and out.

"Are you okay?" she shouted. Connie nodded once as she clung to the brick behind her, closed her eyes, and moved another inch to her left.

# IF THE SHOE FITS, WEAR IT
## By Pong Louie

"Gung-Ping, what's wrong? Why are you sitting here by yourself?"

Gung-Ping Yan looked up at Mr. Ho. His broad shoulders still slumped against the edge of the cafeteria table, his legs stretched out into the aisle. His coarse black hair was long and stuck out here and there, almost like a pad of steel wool that's been pulled apart.

"What's it to you? I'm not doing anything wrong," Gung-Ping shot back.

"No, I'm just concerned about you," Mr. Ho explained.

"Well, there's nothing to be concerned about. I just felt like sitting here." Gung-Ping looked around the Bunker Hill High School cafeteria at the other students chatting with each other. Maybe two dozen national flags hung from the ceiling, each one from a country represented in the student body.

A barely audible bell sounded above the din of four hundred or so students talking at once. As Gung-Ping got up, he admitted to himself that there was something wrong. Why can't I just fit in? he asked himself. I'm a jook-sing, born here in the US, but the other jook-sings think I'm too Chinese to be one of them. Now, if I'm too Chinese, then why do the jook-koks, who immigrated here years ago, think I'm not Chinese enough? Besides, I'm Chinese, so how can I be too Chinese?

As Gung-Ping walked past Mr. Ho, he noticed that this teacher, who seemed to be everyone's friend, must have looked a lot like himself when he was a teenager, medium height, coarse black hair, broad shoulders and thin, although Mr. Ho was a little chubby now.

"Gung-Ping," Mr. Ho interrupted his thoughts. "I know something is bothering you. Anytime you want to talk, I'm available."

Gung-Ping nodded slightly and continued on to his next class. He spent the last two periods thinking about not fitting in. It was obvious to him that if he couldn't fit in with other Chinese, it would be even more difficult for him to fit in with the lo-fan, as Americans are known.

After school, Gung-Ping took the school bus to North Station as he did every day. But instead of taking the Green line to Brighton to go home, he took the Orange line. Still lost in thought, Gung-Ping missed his stop, realizing it only as the train pulled away from the platform. The white signs that announced Chinatown in black letters became blurred as the train picked up speed, screeching and squealing.

Oh well, no big deal. I'll just get off at the next stop, Gung-Ping told himself. It's close enough and I won't have to walk through the Combat Zone. Gung-Ping always hated walking through Boston's adult entertainment district with all the pimps, johns, drunks panhandling and, of course, the prostitutes asking every male passerby, "Hi, do you want a date?" That's the depressing low-life.

The train jerked to a stop at the Medical Center station and the doors slid open. Gung-Ping got off and went up stairs, squinting against the bright sun. He turned the corner and saw, as often was the case, a block of hurdles. For some reason, Don Bosco High School's track team liked to practice jumping hurdles on the sidewalk.

Gung-Ping crossed the street and he could see the massive I-Beam frame of the building going up at the corner of Washington and Oak Streets a block away. Must be another Medical Center building, he told himself. Where am I going anyway? Without an answer, Gung-Ping ambled along Oak Street. From the corner, he could see a dark blue banner hanging across the middle of the next block. The big white letters demanded "No Garage on Oak Street!" in Chinese and English.

Across Washington Street, Oak Street narrows into a one lane, one-way street. On the corner, with construction sites on either side of him, a Chinese man with a pock-marked face was giving out leaflets. Gung-Ping ignored him and kept walking. At the other end of the street was another man doing the same thing. Even with his back to Gung-Ping, he looked familiar.

"Mr. Ho, what are you doing here?" Gung-Ping asked in surprise. Mr. Ho handed him a leaflet. "The hospital wants to build an eight story, four hundred fifty-five car garage over there." Mr. Ho pointed down the street behind Gung-Ping.

"Oh, so that's what that building is," Gung-Ping said.

"No, that's something else. The garage would be next to it," Mr. Ho explained.

"On this little street, next to a day care center? Half a block from the elderly housing and elementary school? Are they crazy?" Gung-Ping couldn't believe it.

"That's right. The City gave the hospital the land where that building is being built in exchange for the land next to it. They promised to return that small piece of land to Chinatown so we could build a community center, but now the City is going back on its word."

"That's not fair! The hospital's already taken a lot of Chinatown's land. They already have a garage on Tremont Street and lots of parking lots," Gung-Ping complained.

"Not only that, the land is in Chinatown, so the people who live here should have a say in what happens to it. So you see why we're fighting it? If you have time, you should come help out. There'll be a community meeting next Tuesday, six-thirty, at the Josiah Quincy School."

"I hate meetings," Gung-Ping said.

"That's okay. You don't have to come to the meeting. You can help in other ways. It's better than sitting around moping."

"All right, I'll see," Gung-Ping said and crossed Harrison Avenue. He read the leaflet as he strolled on to nowhere.

On Tyler Street, half way up the next block, stood "The Bubble", an inflatable building behind a colorfully painted wooden wall that served as Chinatown's YMCA. As he passed by, Gung-Ping thought about the kids inside playing video games and basketball. Recreation, but not a life, he told himself.

A block away, the gang kids were hanging around on the sidewalk and in the parking lot across the street, leaning against cars. No, that's definitely not for me, Gung-Ping thought.

He looked around at the restaurants and all the

restaurant workers standing around waiting for vans to come take them to far-off restaurants, but he knew that he didn't want to work in a restaurant.

So where do I fit in? he asked himself.

At the corner of Harrison Avenue and Beach Street, a young woman with short hair and a cute face was about to offer Gung-Ping a leaflet when she said, "Oh, you already have one," in a squeaky voice.

Gung-Ping moved the hand holding the leaflet slightly, muttered "Yup" and headed toward the Green line on Boylston Street.

Sure are a lot of people doing this stuff, Gung-Ping thought as he looked at the leaflet again. Even Mr. Ho, and he's probably right. It's better than sitting around moping. Maybe I'll go on Tuesday and check it out.

Over the weekend, the more he thought about it, the angrier Gung-Ping became; angry at the hospital, angry at the City.

A hospital's main concern should be health, yet the Medical Center's own proposal endangers the health and safety of the community around it, especially kids and the elderly and how could the City agree to it? Gung-Ping reasoned.

Tuesday evening, Gung-Ping looked around the Quincy School cafeteria in amazement. Mr. Ho was there, along with the guy with the pock-marked face and the woman with short hair. So were about two hundred others. There were people of all ages, residents and suburbanites, jook-sing, jook-kok, lo-fan and representatives from dozens of community organizations. They all got along and worked together. People made him feel welcomed. They accepted him for what he was. There was no jook-sing/jook-kok thing, no tong-yan (Chinese)/lo-fan thing.

They talked about a petition, picket and rally, banners, leaflets, news conference, letter writing campaign, newspaper articles, referendum and fundraising, among other things.

Gung-Ping was so impressed that he signed up to help with the petition, picket and rally, leafleting and fundraising. As he wrote his name and phone number over and over on different sheets of paper, he wondered if there was anything wrong with using the old saying, "If the shoe fits, wear it." in this case, for the shoe certainly seemed to fit comfortably.

# PERFECT BUBBLES
By Yvonne Ng


Hoping for a different outcome
But stuck using the same formula
Love, connect, move, hurt = fail

Because the times in between
Pull, push, shove, and coax
Aggressively gentle
Unabashedly surreptitious

Wait, wait, move
Wait, wait, still

Sprint passionately to the
Next roadblock and hope
Stifle, breathe, a wish
Rewound but it's the same
Wish whispered, repeated, chanted

Hoping that the hum sinks
The perfect bubbles.

*Divergent*

# DOGS IN CHINA
By Gay Eng

There was a time quite a few years ago when the Chinese justified their eating of dog meat by saying Americans also ate dogs.

"What about your hot dogs?" My students would ask. "What's wrong with eating dogs, anyway?"

I would gently have to explain that hot dogs contained no dogs. They consisted of various leftover parts of cows or pigs with spices and chemical preservatives. I had to admit they were quite tasty. But dogs would never be eaten. Dogs are considered Man's Best Friend.

They would look puzzled.

"How can a dog be your friend? They just eat all your food."

Now, on a recent trip to China, the country has caught up if not surpassed the rest of the world in some ways. And in the cities, dogs have indeed become cherished pets.

However, I was even more astounded by the ubiquitous presence of American-style hot dogs, especially at major tourist attractions. Wasn't this blasphemy? Doesn't China have its own rich cuisine and tasty street food? Fried scorpions, fresh crepes stuffed with eggs and scallions, crunchy sea horses, meat and vegetable steamed buns, to name a few. Weren't these street foods much better than the lowly hot dog?

As I was pondering the values and morals of those who would eat hot dogs in China, my Americanized China-born mother remarked that hot dogs in China were different—the skins were much tougher.

"What? When did you have a hot dog?"

"On the Great Wall," she stated matter of factly. "I was waiting for you to climb down from the tower and I got hungry."

She didn't even try to pretend she thought they were lopcheung. Over sixty years ago on the slow boat from Hong Kong to San Francisco, she had a terrible time with the bland American food. One day, the kids in the next bunk came running down and excitedly told all the grownups in steerage that lopcheung were being served. To my Mom's great disappointment, they turned out to be good ol' American hot dogs.

# SHORT
## By Yvonne Ng

Kali Goon didn't mind bending down five inches to kiss her new boyfriend Stanley Lin on his lusciously plump lips. She didn't mind that she could breathe over his head and nary a hair from his halo of soft curls moved out of place.

If she had her way, she'd be with Stanley all the time, but instead she would day dream about him. She dreamt about swimming naked and free in the glorious recesses of his adorable dimples. She'd then cascade down his smooth chest to dangle with ecstasy on his nipple.

The looks and the giggles they'd receive whenever they strolled hand in hand in the park felt like caresses of delicious jealousy because they were destined for couplehood. Besides, she could feel Stanley walk tall with her.

Whenever Kali was with Stanley, she reveled in his jokes, glowed at his touch, and shivered from juicy desire.

She never noticed that he checked his watch so frequently, bolted to help a client, or looked on edge whenever they'd meet in Chinatown for dinner.

She didn't think it was odd that Stanley would go away on frequent business trips or forget to call her when he returned. She accepted that he was an accountant in demand and that he knew best because he was, after all, more educated and well traveled than she.

One day as Kali walked to the grocer on Tyler Street by Essex, she saw shock, dirt, and tears on

Stanley's face as he looked at her between the legs of the two women fighting above him. He lay still on the sidewalk. Each woman heatedly claimed she was his wife. One was swinging a baseball bat that looked like it had just come in contact with his legs. Kali never thought she'd see Stanley this way, and apparently neither did he.

*This short story is dedicated to the AARW Writers' Group. We all encourage each other to publish our work and this piece was entered into a writing contest. It was one of 42 short stories published by the Harvard Book Store as a collection called, "Microchondria."*

# EVER NORTHWARD
## By Alison Chan

First, the silk obi, half untied. Then, the smooth banister of oak wood, darkened with age. Last, the window to the other world.

Scent of cardamom and musk mixes with raw leather and his pheromonal palette, seduction beneath the waxing moon.

Blood spills from the wound she sustained against the frosted glass. Warmth flushes her body, her mind. She can no longer distinguish between the pain, the fear, and her overwhelming desire.

Her dark locks fan across the pillow. When she closes her eyes she sees the ghosts of past passions, those ancient songs of love, the ocean where she first kissed him. A different him.

Where does blood finish and water begin?

"I want..." she says, but it is a thought she cannot complete. What she wants is too complicated, too vast, too nebulous to articulate. He would not understand.

The cracked mirror. The shadow in the wings. The melancholy words scrawled on the last page of her journal. <u>Nathanael is gone. I shall not look behind me. Only forward. Northward.</u>

With a glance, he questions her.

This time, she does not say no.

# CANOEING
By Pong Louie

Damn, it's hot, Al thought as he came out of the dinky little general store with his cigarettes and matches. A station-wagon was driving down the road with a canoe strapped to its roof. A soccer mom car driven by a guy, must be a fag, Al thought. As the car drove by, its mirror slightly nicked the one on AL's car. Al crossed the street and examined the mirror on his 1971 Dodge Charger. There was a tiny scratch in the paint. Al got in his car and followed the wagon. A few miles down the road, the wagon pulled onto a path leading to the river. Al watched as they took the canoe off the roof and put it halfway into the water, then he drove to the next landing area, where it was rockier.

Al parked and took everything out of his pockets. He lit a cigarette and walked down to the river and looked upstream. After ten minutes, the canoe came into sight. About time! Here goes, Al said to himself and slipped carefully into the river. He swam out to the middle, near where the rocks jutted way out. When the canoe came close, he took a deep breath and ducked under the water.

\* \* \* \* \* \* \* \* \* \*

Bob's a/c wasn't working in his beat-up old car and beads of sweat were rolling down his face. His black Trans Am was nothing like Michael Knight's KITT anymore. As he drove along the narrow road, he noticed a little path leading down to the river with a '71 Charger parked on the side of the road. Wow!, he thought, I haven't seen one of these in a couple of decades now. He pulled up behind the Charger and got out to check it out. It had been meticulously restored, all original, with no silly modifications. He wanted to talk to the owner, so he walked down the path to try to find him. He felt sure it was a he and not a she who was driving the car. As he reached the river bank, Bob noticed a canoe flipping over, spilling its 2 paddlers. He wondered if the people were OK or if they needed help. But wait! What's going on? He saw a third person, who was grabbing the canoe-ers. But he wasn't helping them! He was trying to push them down and push them into the rocks. Bob quickly kicked off his shoes and dove into the river, swimming under water out to the canoe. He kicked hard to resurface quickly with his fist aimed at the guy's groin. The guy exhaled loudly and doubled over. Bob followed with a kick to the face and the guy started choking in the water. Bob quickly put his arms out under the two victims' chests and kicked off the guy's butt, back peddling back to shore. No longer interested in talking to the Charger's owner, Bob led the two strangers straight to his car, leaving his shoes behind. He locked the doors and drove off, before talking to them, afraid the guy, so big and muscular, might somehow be able to recover quickly enough and come after them.

"OK, it should be safe now." He burned rubber as he pulled away. "What the hell's going on? Why was that guy trying to kill you? Let's find the police. Where's your car?" Bob couldn't stop asking questions, as he tried to catch his breath and calm down.

"Diu kui lo mo! Kui che lun seen geh. Moon bak see seung saht ngo dei. Doh mm jee mut yeh see fat sung geh. Mm go kui jow gah geh. Mm hai nei gao ngo dei, ah, say gung ah. Ding kui ge fai!" Bob had no idea what the guy was saying, but could tell that he was upset, and rightfully so.

"I sorry husband no speak English. Sank you very much help us. I sink man crazy try kill us. We not know why. Car is other way. We try talk police."

# LAO FAHN*
## By Yvonne Ng

Angela Lee's smile was wide and toothy. She and her best friend Peggy Ma were going to finally move into their new two-bedroom apartment in Flushing, Queens. It wasn't much of a space but to two young recent college graduates, it was freedom, independence, and splendid.

Angela had taken curtain measurements for the windows. The view was directly level with the sidewalk. Shoes, car tires and occasional paws floated by. There wasn't much natural light because the basement apartment had only four windows but that suited the two just fine. Peggy had already spied three electrical outlets. Angela was quite tall and would have to bend a little whenever she'd enter the tiny kitchen.

The apartment find had been a result of Peggy's sister's boyfriend, Way Lun. He seemed to know just about everyone in the neighborhood and gave them pointers of where to shop and catch the train. Way Lun came along to help translate because Peggy and Angela's Chinese was a bit rusty.

Happy and thrilled, both women chatted about how they'd decorate as they headed toward the Chinese bakery to hand over the $900 deposit and first month's rent to Mrs. Wong, the landlord. The bakery was busy so Peggy and Angela had to wait but Mrs. Wong glanced at Angela every so often with a grimace.

Way Lun called to Mrs. Wong, who looked at Angela and inspected her from head to toe. She said something in rapid Chinese and kept shaking her head. Angela could pick out the familiar words, "ng A" and "lao fahn".

Way Lun was arguing with Mrs. Wong trying to explain Angela was just a "jook san" but good and reliable. Mrs. Wong wouldn't budge. Angela, who was standing closest to Mrs. Wong, stared at her with hurt and anger. She said, "ngoi ng hi lao fahn" and turned and walked out of the bakery. Angela didn't want to give Mrs. Wong the satisfaction of seeing her tears.

*foreigner
ng A = don't give
jook san = hollow bamboo
ngoi ng hi lao fahn = I'm not a foreigner

# BUCKY
By Gay Eng


I shot the sheriff. I didn't mean to, but he was in the way. Bucky and I were ten and we were only foolin' around. He found his Pa's pistol and we went behind the garage. Someone must have heard the shots. We shot at some old cans and bottles. Big deal. It's not like there were people around. Bucky and I, we've been friends since kindergarten. He lived across the street from our restaurant, and my family lived above it. We both learned to fish and ride bikes at the same time.

Anyway, here we were with nothin' to do on a summer afternoon. So we went out back and started shooting. Bucky wasn't a very good shot. As a matter of fact, he missed all the cans. I hit two out of five. We got tired of shooting. We were hot and sticky and lay down in the grass. Suddenly, Bucky rolled over and kissed me. I pushed him away. I didn't want him slobbering all over me. What was he doing anyway? It was the first time he treated me like a girl. My heart was pounding. We were best friends. Now he'd gone and wrecked everything. I ran away from him, picking up the pistol from the grass. I thought of shooting him. Just then, the sheriff drove up, jumped out of the car, and ran over in front of me. I swear, the pistol just went off. I don't know what happened. The next thing I know I'm in the deputy's car, with Bucky looking wide-eyed at me, saying, "Wow, you get to ride in the sheriff's car."

They wouldn't let Bucky visit me in the cell. He had hopped on his bike and ridden as fast as he could to the county sheriff's. They actually were taking my fingerprints when Bucky came in. By that time I was crying. I knew I would get a good whuppin' at home. Baba hardly ever hit me. But when he did, I knew I had been bad. Ma would just give me the silent treatment. But hey, maybe now I was going to jail for a long time.

# A BLOCK OF WHITE
## By Amanda Chiang

You land upon the plane,
On top of the intruder,
You sit upon him firmly,
Grinding
Crushing
His lean and black-skinned body.

Your tough and tender tendon,
Rubs and overwhelms his black,
You tear him down insistently,
By bit
By piece
'Til no trace of him seen.

You stop and step aside,
A gust of wind sweeps by,
You watch his ashes
scatter,
disappear.
You gloat, for the land is clean and clear.

Only your white suit of armor remains—
stained.

# LIMIT
By Yvonne Ng

When does it hit you?
When your eyes swell from tear after tear of regret and loss?
When you can only remember the caresses of tenderness?
When you think, "I've wasted so many years"?
When you despair or when you hope that things will change?

What will it take to start your renaissance?
The sixth time he says, "I don't love you anymore"?
The sixty-first time you reach out for love and receive nothing?
The six hundredth time he criticizes and belittles you?

When will you realize you deserve someone who loves you, cares for you, does everything in his power to make you happy?

When will you make one of the hardest decisions in your life – to choose you first because you've been in last place for years?

# A WEIRD SUMMER
## By Pong Louie

The late morning July sun was high and hot. Bong Dak Ho walked bouncily along Hillside Avenue to the 179th Street subway station. His T-shirt clung to his thin, tanned body.

'Boy, this summer is getting weirder and weirder,' Bong Dak thought. He flicked his head to the right to get his hair out of his eyes. 'First the work-study job as an artist when I'm not even an artist. Now, I have to work this health fair for a week.'

Bong Dak slowed his normally fast pace a little. 'Eleven blocks is no problem at 8:00, but what time is it now?' He glanced at his old Timex Boy Scout watch and flicked his head again. '11:00. It's too hot now and there's no trees on Hillside. Why don't they do regular work hours? This is a pain.'

At least it's not so crowded now, he thought as he looked around the platform. Seated on the F train as it clanged and squealed away from the platform, Bong Dak tried to put the nauseating subway smell out of his mind. He reviewed the circumstances that led to his present predicament.

Three days ago, he had taken the bus uptown, as he did every Friday, to deliver his week's work to his supervisor on the fourth floor of the public health building.

"Bong, you always bring the work so nicely wrapped," Mr. Plotsky had commented as he unwrapped the package. "Beautiful, this is great work."

"Thanks."

Mr. Plotsky had run his hand over his shiny bald head and stuck it into his pants pockets. Then he dropped the bomb. "Bong, next week your assignment will be a little different."

"Okay."

"You see, the Chinatown Health Clinic will be sponsoring a health fair next week. They need help, so I'm sending you since you're bilingual. All right?"

"Ah… yeah, sure," Bong Dak said and wondered why he was answering a rhetorical question.

"Now the health fair will be at The Hamilton-Madison House. I'll tell you how to get there."

"Oh, I know where it is," Bong Dak said, but thought to himself, I just don't want to go there again.

"Good. You report there Monday at noon. You'll work 12:00 to 8:00 next week. You should talk to Gina Li. She'll be in charge."

"Okay."

"Come back here the following Monday and I'll give you your new assignment then."

"Okay."

Bong Dak came back to the present as the N train pulled into the Canal Street station. He got off the train, not remembering changing to the N from the F. He flicked his head and went up stairs. He squinted against the bright sun as he came out of the station.

'Ahh, that's better,' Bong Dak thought when he turned off Canal onto Mott Street. 'There's no trees here either, but at least the buildings block some of the sun.'

On the other side of Chatham Square was a man selling hot dogs from a beat-up old cart with a faded umbrella over it. Bong Dak bought three hot dogs with mustard and sauerkraut. He flicked his hair out of his eyes and walked down Oliver Street to The Hamilton-Madison House. He steeled himself, prepared mentally to enter the settlement house again. His first time since his father died two years ago. He prepared to again see those Golden Age Center people his father had directed for so many years.

Bong Dak was here to work. He didn't need people telling him how much his father meant to them or how much they missed him. He didn't want them to remind him of what a shame it was that a great man like his father died at the age of fifty-four. He dreaded reliving his father's death. He also didn't want to be compared to his father. How could he ever live up to his father's legacy?

Upon entering The Hamilton-Madison House, Bong Dak saw the back of a tall, thin man walking up the stairs. He had short hair, allowing the ends of his glasses to show. 'Now what?' he asked himself. 'Let him be and he won't even know I'm here... but he's sure to find out, then he'd be upset that I didn't say hello.'

"Cheung Sang!" he called to Mr. Cheung in Chinese.

Bob Cheung, now director of the Golden Age Center, stopped and turned around. He looked confused as he studied the person who had called him, then his face lit up with recognition.

"Bong Dak!" He started back down the stairs with his right hand extended, "How are you? What are you doing here?"

Bong Dak shook his hand, "I'm OK. I'm here to help with the health fair. How are you?

"I'm fine. Let me go get Mary." Bob rushed away

and came back dragging a woman by the hand. Bong Dak immediately recognized the short, round-faced woman as Mrs. Cheung.

"Bong Dak, ho ma? How are you, long time no see."

"Cheung Tai," Bong Dak greeted her, "Nice to see you two again." Bong Dak glanced at his watch and said, "I have to report to work now. I'll talk to you two later." OK, that wasn't so bad, he thought as he hurried away to look for Gina Li.

Bong Dak saw a young woman, at most five feet tall, rushing around, telling people where to go and what to do. Her flowing waist-length hair swished back and forth as she moved.

"Hi, are you Gina Li?"

"Yep."

"I'm Bong Dak Ho. I'm…"

"Oh, good. Here's the schedule posted on the wall. You'll be upstairs in Room 1, where they're doing skin and prostate exams. You can eat your hot dogs there and I'll be up soon to show everyone what to do." Gina started to move on, then stopped, "Oh, you don't have to bring lunch. We'll be supplying lunch later on, around 3:00."

Bong Dak was glad he'd bought the hot dogs. Three was much too late for lunch. He'd starve. He looked at the schedule and thought, Oh man, come on. Who said I was working Saturday? I'll have to talk to her about that.

Upstairs, taped to the first door he saw, was a hand-written sign that read, "Room 1: Skin and Prostate Exams" in English, Chinese and Spanish. I coulda printed a sign for them in English and Spanish. It'd look better, Bong Dak thought. He walked through the doorway and the stuffy, musty, hot air hit him like a wall. "Oh, can't breathe. When's the last time they used this room?" he muttered as he walked back out. He sat on a bench in the hallway and ate his hot dogs.

Great! I hate paper work  I hate sitting around all day. Why me? Bong Dak thought after Gina's explanation of what they had to do. She rushed off without giving Bong Dak a chance to talk to her about the schedule. Well, I guess I'll have to get used to it. I'm stuck here for the week, he thought.

Bong Dak and the three Chinese volunteers worked all afternoon, continuously filling out forms as people filed in. The Hispanic kid took care of the occasional Spanish-speaking person. The four volunteers worked enthusiastically.

It was almost three when they finally got a break and Bong Dak was able to talk to the volunteers. The muscular, wavy-haired kid was José, a Puerto Rican-American teen participating in some sort of summer program. The round guy with thick glasses was Ricky, an immigrant from Hong Kong and pre-med at Columbia. John was a tall, thin bag salesman trying to go to med school. The chubby, bright-eyed teen was Bill, who had just graduated from high school, planning to be pre-med.

"Everyone's pre-med. What am I doing here? Bong Dak said.

"Not me," said José.

"Yeah, but you're still in high school," Bong Dak commented.

"So what's your major? Bill asked.

"Me? I don't know anymore. It was M.E. last year. All I know now is that it won't be pre-med.

"So if you're not interested in medicine, why are you interested in doing this? John asked.

"It's not interest." Bong Dak answered and explain why he was there.

"Oh, so you're like me, you got sent here, but you get paid and I don't," José commented.

"Yeah, …"

"Bong Dak," Mr. Cheung interrupted.

Bong Dak got up and flicked the hair out of his eyes as he walked out of the room.

"So what's up with you now? Mr. Cheung asked.

"Well, I just finished my first year at NYU and I'm here for the week."

"How's your mother?"

"She's doing OK. It's been hard, but she's surviving."

"And what about your sisters?"

"They're OK too. Mei Ling got married a couple of months ago and Mei Ying just graduated from Brandeis and has a government job."

"Wow, that's great and I'm glad to see you doing some volunteer work."

"Actually, I'm not. I have a work-study job for the Health Department and they sent me here. To be honest, I didn't really want to come, but after three hours with those guys, it's not so bad. I'm starting to understand why they volunteered."

"Yes, once you've done some community work, you're addicted. No matter how much you hate the tasks, you feel good about it and that it's all worthwhile."

"Ah Bong Dak ah." It was his aunt, or more accurately, his father's cousin's wife.

"Biao Moo," Bong Dak greeted her.

"Good thing you're here. Of course I don't know English, but they don't even understand my Taishanese. Come help me."

Bong Dak's aunt had always gotten by with the Taishan dialect, so she never bothered to learn Cantonese. But now, she was dealing with American born Chinese who didn't know any Chinese and Hong Kong immigrants who knew only Cantonese and English.

Now, Bong Dak not only felt useful, he also felt special. When Gina came around at the end of the day, he decided it wasn't necessary to talk to her about Saturday. Gina was looking for volunteers to help with a mobile blood testing/screening that the Health Center would be doing in two weeks. Bong Dak signed up to help after work. This time he would be a real volunteer.

# ODE TO THE PHENOMENAL WOMEN IN MY LIFE
By Yvonne Ng

Today, I was thinking about you and how you are a phenomenal woman.

You are a constant inspiration because...

You give yourself lovingly to your family and friends.

You always share your wisdom with grace and tact (most of the time).

Your strength and courage are unfailing even when you feel they are short in supply.

Your humor is infectious and uplifts everyone around you.

You listen always.

You have a signature dish that's dang delicious.

You are a hero just about every day.

Please know that you are loved and that even when you are feeling low or frustrated, you've got me and others cheering for you, praying for you, wishing you only the best.

You are a phenomenal woman.
And I'm grateful to have you in my life.

# DEATH
By Amanda Chiang


A silent black
Magnet

# *Radiant*

# LIFE FROM THE VIEWPOINT OF A CHINATOWN CHICKEN
By Cynthia Yee

I lay here, all fragrant and beautifully dressed, listening to the sound of happy chatter and laughter all around me. My head and graceful neck rest neatly by my side and my slender legs are carefully tucked under me. I feel so very elegant. I am the center of a festive occasion. The smell of burning incense swirl around me and a great fuss accompany the aromas. I have never felt this important in all my Chicken Life.

I was once alive, albeit some might say, what kind of Life is that, squawking around, scratching the ground and pecking at pieces of grain? But it was a Life, nevertheless. I ate. I defecated. And I pecked at lesser ones in the yard.

One day all that suddenly changed. I was packed into a crate with others of my kind and trucked to a place full of squawking birds held in cages. Ended were my days of freedom on the farm, walking about, head held high, strutting my stuff. We were crowded into cages of twelve or more. I pecked at the grain in the trough and, of course, at those lesser than me. It was, after all, my nature to do so.

One sunny, snowy, and cold winter morning, a little girl with shiny, straight black hair came into the place where we stayed. "A six pound pullet, please." she said. I saw a hand reach into my cage and I felt it grab my neck. Off to the inner chambers I went. They slit my throat and drained my blood and then removed my beautiful, shiny frock of feathers... Ugh! A powerful spray of water finished me off. I was then thrown into a brown paper bag.

The little girl hugged me close to her chest as she walked. She snuggled me closer and tighter. To keep warm, I think. My body, you see, still contained the warmth of Life. I snuggled back. I have never been hugged before in my entire Chicken Life.

I felt us climbing up steep stairs and then into a steamy apartment kitchen where two women enthusiastically greeted us. "Ai-ya! Ai ya!" they exclaimed with big smiles. I was bathed and massaged with a nice salt-water bath. I have never had one before, you see. A bath, that is. And a massage for that matter. I giggled to myself as they rubbed me all over with aromatic bean sauces. Suddenly whoops! They tucked a clove of garlic, a scallion and a piece of tangerine rind inside me. What a strange feeling. Into a wok and onto a rack I went. Hot steam enveloped me Ahhh...pretty nice on a cold snowy day. Over an hour passed and before I realized it, I was cooked!

Before the great feast could begin, I was placed on a table in front of a window. Three porcelain bowls filled with rice wine, three pairs of ivory chopsticks, three porcelain spoons, six sticks of incense stuck into a can of sand, a plate of shiny oranges, sweet and savory rice cakes, and a slab of roast pork were lined up around me... They poured the rice wine on the floor and made a few cuts, removing my wing. Each person bowed three times in front of me facing the window and the open sky.

Wow...They say I am a Special Offering to Heaven, Earth, and Man and to all the family's Ancestors.

Me, lowly me, a lowly chicken from a dusty farm yard and a dirty cage. Who could ever have guessed such a special honor would be bestowed on a lowly chicken? Incense perfumed the air as the woman and man chanted good wishes, praise to the gods and ancestors, and made humble requests for a prosperous year, healthy lives, and obedient children.

I felt myself carried on an aluminum tray into the kitchen where they chopped me into bite-size pieces. I was put back together all whole again on a beautiful porcelain plate and brought to a table surrounded by eager and happy people. The little girl with the shiny black hair and a boy younger than her, fought over my heart but the girl won by decision of the older members. She was older than him by two years and therefore worthy of respect and deference, they said. So my heart became her. As a consolation, the boy received my crunchy gizzard and they happily shared my tasty liver between them. My tail of glistening yellow fat was served to the eldest person as a sign of respect for their old age because it is nice and soft and easy to chew. The youngest children were awarded my drumsticks and wings so they might grow strong and fly high and far someday. Then my dark back pieces were offered to each other as a sign of courtesy for that meat is considered the choicest. My sweet graceful neck was the favorite for the women. My white breast was offered to the girl and boy. The elders, laughing, said that they are American children so they would like the white meat. The children refused, knowing that it was considered the least tasty. They knew only foolish people would choose that.

And so, thus, I became part of the family and energized their labors and their studies and blessed their efforts. And by so doing, I contributed to the World's progress and a family's hopes and dreams for the future.

*First published in the Asian American Resource Workshop Newsletter. Based on my happy memories of many delicious family meals growing up on Hudson Street in Boston's Chinatown with my dear little cousin, Albert, our parents, sojourner uncles and paper brothers and sisters-in-law and of course, our wonderful Chinatown playmates. This is dedicated to them and, of course, to the delicious Chinatown chickens, I say thank you for keeping me warm through all those cold and snowy winter mornings.*

# REFLECTION
## By Amanda Chiang

On the metro
underground
I sit beside my grandpa
Next to Him
in the window
I see His reflection
Another side of him

him in the window
so far away
I can not touch
can not feel
his thoughts I can not reach
his past I can not know

him in the window
so close
so far

he right next to me
so close
so far

# JAPANESE NAMES
By Karen S. Young


Masanori Hongo

Lina Hoshino

Molly Kitajima

Stephanie Miyashiro

Jimi Yamaichi

The bus monitor read the names
Japanese names, beautiful names pronounced correctly every time we got on and off the bus to Tule Lake. It was a list of names to make sure we didn't leave anyone behind at rest stops, but to me --- it felt like a roll call of honor.

Daisuke Ito

Hiroshi Kashiwagi

Don Misumi

Peter Yamamoto

Pam Yoshido

How many times in my lifetime have I heard names like these mispronounced, demolished, obliterated ..... disrespected? In my school classroom.

In line at the restaurant. At the airport check in counter. At the doctor's office. Mr. uh, Mrs. Ha ---, Hase ...., Haga ..., Hasebaga

Anna Hasegawa

Betsy Hasegawa

Carol Hasegawa
And how many times ... HOW many times have I heard 'oh, that's all right', 'oh, it's okay, just call me Mrs. H.'
The bus monitor read the names
Japanese names, beautiful names pronounced correctly EVERY time we got on and off the bus to Tule Lake. Tears running down my face, I sat and listened. It was like music -- perfect rhythm, gorgeous cadence ...

Satsuki Ina

Karen Fuji

Sharon Nakamura

Stan Shikuma

Jan Yoshiwara

# FOUND IN A FLICKER
by Yvonne Ng


Kali saw something at the water's edge and jumped back with a squeak. It was a rusted can of tuna with the waffle top languidly waving back and forth right below the surface. She probably wouldn't have noticed except the filtered sun glinted against the perfect profile of St. Anthony of Padua that bloomed on the lid. The Patrician nose, soft smile and gentle wreath of hair that surrounded his dome, this image of St. Anthony seemed to shed relief and hope.

Kali dropped to her knee and reached for the can. Tadpoles had taken up residence but Kali gently evicted them. As she brought the can closer, she could see the Patron Saint of lost items and lost souls more clearly with a halo glowing around his head.

Kali immediately placed the can onto the grass and knelt in front of it, completely ignoring the strollers, joggers, tourists, moms with baby carriages, and bikers that passed by enjoying their day on the Charles.

Kali bowed her head, made a sign of the cross, and said a prayer of thanks for happening upon this beautiful can. She sensed this small empty vessel was shrouded in a mystical power, because she couldn't remember ever feeling so overjoyed, contented, and at peace. Oddly, it smelled like a cinnamon banana smoothie.

She thought about how others could marvel at this

treasure and appreciate it too. But before she could carefully wrap the can in her nylon recyclable bag, an enormous seagull swooped down from the sky and took off with the can across the water.

Kali screamed in surprise and anger. She stood helpless as the seagull flew away with the can in his beak towards the Zakim Bridge. Just as she was about to curse the bird, she felt a strange tug in her pant pocket. Reaching in, her fingers closed in on her grandmother's ring – a ring she had thought she lost three years ago. Kali dropped back onto her knees and said a prayer of thanks (and forgiveness for her mean thoughts about the seagull).

# HOT
By Gay Eng

Searing heat,
He stirs
The fire red pepper in the sizzling oil,
Shanghai greens tossed against
Slippery iron slopes.
As the burnt soy smell of twice
cooked beef crawl
into the front room,
I sit typing
beside the window
with the gray pounding rain,
A hint of sesame in the air.

Dark swirling clouds in the distance
Maybe the heat will
let up,
I've just got to finish
this story,
my mind on the action
scene, the car chase,
the murder weapon.
When suddenly the sky is
an eerie green
and I hear the roar of a train,
But there are no tracks,
I think as I stumble to the basement,
His strong hands pushing and grabbing
From behind.

# IF HUDSON STREET COULD TALK
## By Cynthia Yee

*An edited excerpt from an essay by Cynthia Yee, a former Hudson Street resident displaced by the construction of the Central Artery.*

*"The past lives on; in art and memory, but it is not static: it shifts and changes as the present throws its shadows backwards. The landscape also changes, but far more slowly; it is a living link between what we were and what we have become."*

*Margaret Drabble, A Writers Britain*

The tall gray concrete wall looms and casts its shadow over the edge of Chinatown. It faces Tai Tung Village and what is left of the red brick townhouses of Hudson Street. New arrivals and the younger generation see the wall as always having been there supporting the ramp leading to the Southeast Expressway; the ramp built so South Shore people could get home faster from their downtown jobs. Weeds now grow taller than me and there are bits of graffiti on the wall. Vagrants loiter on the corner of Harvard Street near the old YMCA. I hesitate, and almost turn back, but decide to walk ahead to the end; more weeds and a chain link fence overlooking more expressway.

This now eerily quiet street was once rich with the chanting games and laughter of children and the activity of families; it was an island of fun and safety. Hudson Street was the main residential neighborhood of Chinatown in the 1950's and early 1960's. It was populated with Syrian families and new immigrants from Hoi San, a rural area of Guangdong Province in Southern China. The children were mostly the first post- WW II generation to be born here in America. Occasionally, new brides arrived from Hong Kong bringing fancy silks, jewelry and decorative, fragrant cedar chests we so admired. In those days, mothers were home usually stitching piecework, 50 cents per shirt for Collegetown Sportswear Co. Fathers slept until noon and went to work at 2:00 p.m. in the restaurants across Kneeland Street, the crucial divide between residential and commercial life. It was a commonly accepted rule that we were to play quietly outdoors until noon so as not to disturb the fathers who had returned from work at 2:00 and sometimes 3:00 in the morning.

I was born while my parents lived at No.133 Hudson and we moved to No. 116 across the street when I was a baby. There I spent my childhood on the upper end of Hudson Street, now all gone. At one end of the block was an abandoned gas station where we played "house" using the foundations of old gas pumps as stoves and the wild dandelions and ailanthus tree leaves as vegetables. At the other end of the block was a Syrian grocery shop in the basement where aromatic smells of pine nuts and olives in great big wooden barrels permeated the air. I used to watch the Syrian women ladling out the olives, of which there was a great variety, and tasting them. I wished I could do so, too. At Jimmy's Spa on the same corner we bought big ice cream cones for 10 cents. Vanilla, chocolate and strawberry were the only flavors. It was there I learned that tragedy would be ameliorated with kindness. When my scoop of ice cream fell onto the ground with my first lick, I stared at it with disappointment. But Jimmy gave me another big scoop accompanied by a big smile. I always remembered that act of kindness from one of the very few non-Chinese persons I came in contact with.

Shared streets and shared toys were our life. A volleyball net strung across the street; one pair of bicycles belonging to a brother and sister but shared by all; games of stick-ball in the Quincy schoolyard; hopscotch; kick-the-can in the middle of the street; climbing the wrought iron fence of the Syrian church at the upper end to get to the outfield, and most remembered of all, "Bak bak bak Lo Si Bak. How many fingers have I got up?" At dinner time, mothers hung out of their windows to call children home to meals. "Hep-pa, hek fahn ah!" was echoed by Hep-pa's playmates in translation " Hey, Hep, your Mom wants you for dinner!"

Night time was playtime on the streets in the summer as mothers conversed on stoops and it was too hot to stay home. Baseball card collections were treasures as we played flip-ups on the stoops. Little square rice bags made by ourselves with rice taken from our mothers' rice bins and scraps of cloth from their sewing were used to play "jacks." Woven clothesline were used as jump ropes when we jumped to rhymes that spelled M-I-S-S-I-S-S-I-P-P-I and other classic American jump rope rhymes, graduating eventually to Double Dutch. Chinese jump ropes were made by linking rubber bands together and what skilled high-jumpers we were!

Sharing everything made more for all. Comics from Carl Martin's Drugstore were 10 cents a piece and 25 cents for the Giant Special. If you were flush with cash, 25 cents for a large box of thick-cut french fries could be bought from the Gam-Sun and Nile restaurants on Hudson Street to be shared with all your friends with lots of ketchup. If you were less flush that day, 5 cents would buy a bag of Wise potato chips which we also shared.

On our father's "day-off" we enjoyed extra special delicious home cooked meals and trips across Kneeland Street to drink chocolate milk while the men talked over cups of coffee. Food was so whole then. Freshly killed chickens, still warm, were carried home to be cooked; whole fish, lobsters, ducks, and pigs were common fare. I was shocked later to discover supermarkets where you could buy packages of frozen animal parts. What was so great about getting a drumstick on your birthday or a wing if there was a whole package of them? It would take the fun out of fighting with your cousin for the chicken heart or liver, of which there was only one of each!

New Year's Eve was the busiest night at the Chinese restaurants where our fathers worked. On New Year's morning, we were to be extra quiet, but my cousin and I would peek at the hats and noisemakers our dads had brought home from the restaurants. And as soon as they woke, we could begin our fun parading around with clangers, clappers, twirlers, blowout zappers and new year hats. It occupied us for hours. The sight of those noisemakers and hats in antique stores would bring back that sweet memory.

Of course, all of us grew up and moved into mainstream American life and went on to successful enough lives. Some of us return to do community work as volunteers, doctors, nurses, teachers and political advocates. Some of us have children

graduating from Ivy League colleges and graduate
programs. Many of these children do not speak
Chinese and some, if not most, have no idea how we
grew up. Lately, I find my peers and myself speaking
of our childhood with sweet nostalgia. We see each
other mostly at the wakes of our parents or the
weddings of our children. As we reminisce and laugh,
we realize we are the only ones that share that
common memory, something no one else could ever
understand. It is at that moment of realization for
each of us at differing times that we begin to feel that
we have moved into another generation, and it
happens so seemingly suddenly that it takes us often
by surprise. And yet, that sweet memory of simple,
youthful play remains. If you were to ask us, former
children of Hudson Street, what it was like to live
there, all of us can remember every house and who
lived in each one, every crack, every rail, every
sidewalk, every pole, every stoop, and every face, for
that was our childhood landscape: always sunny,
always a playmate nearby. The street was ours to
share and on which to create imaginary worlds.

One former child of Hudson Street, when asked,
"What is your key memory of Hudson Street?" broke
into a smile and said, "Being happy!" When asked
"Why?" he replied, "We were with our friends." He
said, "One bottle cap could be made into a game that
would last for hours. We had to use our imagination
and organize ourselves. We were not pawns in
someone else's agenda as children are nowadays."

Cynics may say that we look back on our past with
rose-colored glasses and forget the bad. Life was
imperfect as it always is. Perhaps with age, we
remember what was best. Some may call it a false

nostalgia but as I asked former residents for their key memories, each one broke into a smile.

It is with time and perspective that we can remember best the feelings of a time and place. To me, Hudson Street was a sunny island of caring neighbors, where everyone looked out for each others' children and where we played games of our own invention and making.

Implicit in the freedom we were given was the trust of our parents that we would always do the right thing. It was our home.

*Originally published by the Chinese Historical Society of New England in 2003. Reprinted here with some minor revisions.*

Cousins Cynthia Yee and Albert Yee playing in the snow on Hudson Street, c. 1955. Picture taken by the late Eddie Moon Fun Yee.

The Yee family celebrates a birthday at 116 Hudson Street, c. 1959. Picture taken by the late Eddie Moon Fun Yee.

Cynthia Yee and Ken Lim celebrate their last Easter holiday on Hudson Street in 1962.

# LOVE AND MARCHING
## By Gay Eng

Terry stepped out of the shower in the Foreign Students Dorm and quickly toweled herself dry. There was plenty of hot water now in the early part of the 6 to 9 PM allotted bathing time. She was lucky that she got into the shower right at six when no one else was around. She had the luxury of the shower room to herself and had even locked the door for extra privacy. It was so hard to get time to oneself here. She was really excited about the May Day Dance that she had organized. She couldn't believe that her students had never been to a dance before. Sure, China was just opening up to the rest of the world, but how could they not have dances once in a while? Of course, it wasn't an official dance. It was just a get together for the English Department, of which Terry was an honored teacher.

Terry had a hard time deciding exactly what to wear to this event. She'd probably be deported if she wore a slinky dress. She finally decided to wear a sleeveless, brightly flowered polyester dress she had picked up from the street vendors in Hong Kong. She rubbed her towel over the small fogged-up mirror on the wall and examined her face. Good, no zits. She had large brown almond-shaped eyes and a small nose and mouth, and long black hair. She often attracted admiring glances when she walked down the street in Boston and New York. Here, however, she looked like everyone else. But her foreign clothes and mannerisms often brought uncomfortable stares.

After she finished pulling her dress over her head

and yanked it into place, she unlocked the door. She tried to pull it open, but it wouldn't budge. The doorknob wouldn't turn and she couldn't open the door. She looked around the room in desperation—there was one bathtub with shower in the corner and another stall with a shower. There was a window but she wasn't about to jump out of a third story window even if she could. She tugged and tugged on the door but it still wouldn't move.

She screamed as loud as she could, "Hey, is anybody there? I need help. Help!"

She doubted if anyone could hear her. Beyond this room there was another room, which had a sink and two squat toilets and cubbyholes for personal supplies, and then another closed door. She'd miss the whole dance, which no one except the other foreigners knew was a dance. She was bringing her boom box, and everyone else was bringing their favorite music. She really wanted to dance with Eric. Eric was a tall blonde Swede that she fell in love with at first sight. She didn't even like blondes--boys or girls. Her first day here she was out jogging at seven in the morning and who did she bump into but some other crazy American? Eric was from the University of Minnesota and of Swedish descent so she called him The Swede. She couldn't believe she had traveled six thousand miles from Boston to Beijing, only to fall in love with a Swede from Minnesota. She certainly hadn't told her mother, who was hoping she'd find a nice Chinese boy.

Finally, she opened the window and heard some people talking.

"Hey!" she shouted.

Two guys looked up at her.

"Hey, I need some help."

One of the guys said, "Bu dong. Ting bu dong."

They both hurried away.

"Wait, don't go." Terry cried out. Now she racked her brain for her Chinese and could only remember her mother lecturing her on how she was Chinese and should speak Chinese. Every night her mother would start dinner by ordering them to practice their Chinese. But Terry and her sister would invariably end up calling each other names in broken Chinese and their frustrated mother would be yelling at them. Now, how do you say help? Is it jiu or bong?

She heard some more people outside and shouted, "Jiu wo! Jiu wo!"

Then she heard the familiar voice of one of her students, Mr. Zhang, "Teacher Loo! Teacher Loo! We are coming."

A few minutes later, she heard her student, Zhang, outside the door.

"Teacher Loo! We are here to save you."

"Great, I cannot open the door." Terry shouted. "The door's not locked, but I cannot open it."

She heard some other voices talking in Chinese and then Zhang said, "Teacher, the door broke. We kick open. Stay off."

"Okay, go ahead!"

The door flew open with a loud bang, and there was Zhang and the dorm czar, Comrade Li, along with one of the dorm attendants. Zhang was one of her favorite students. Unlike the others, he often spoke up in class. He helped her with her shopping after class and often brought her little presents, such as apples or pears. He was tall, with a broad honest face and the high cheek bones of most Northerners.

The other students affectionately called him Old or Lao Zhang.

"Oh, thank you! Xie, xie." Terry almost cried with relief. Good thing she remembered to bring all her clothes with her.

Zhang and the others smiled back at her and apologized about the door.

"No problem," she said. "I'm just glad I'm out of there. Thank you, Comrade Li. Thank you everyone."

Comrade Li smiled curtly and then said something in Chinese to Zhang and they quickly hurried away towards the stairs.

"See you at the party!" Terry shouted after them.

Terry hurried back to her room and put the finishing touches on her hair. Instead of tying it back, she decided to let her long black hair hang loose. She was tired of the tight pigtails that she and every other woman wore. She even put on a some eye-liner and mascara. She sat on her bed and looked around the small drab room. At least she had a little balcony and French doors. By Chinese standards, it was luxurious – an eight by ten room for one person. There was a polished wood floor with a thick floral carpet, a single bed, a small wooden desk and chair, a wooden bookcase and an armchair with a tan cloth cover.

Just then, there was a knock at the door. Terry opened the door and Eric pushed her in the room.

"What are you doing here?" Terry whispered.

"I had to see Cinderella before the ball. Very nice." He looked her up and down and laughed.

"Oh, why didn't you get dressed up?" Terry said and frowned at his plain blue Chinese Mao jacket and blue cotton pants.

"No need for me to dress up. I stick out like a sore

thumb no matter what." It was true. At six feet two and with light blonde hair, Eric often drew a crowd when he left the campus.

"Anyway, how did you sneak past the spies?"

"I came on a special mission. I am helping Teacher Loo carry heavy equipment."

Terry laughed. "Yes, and I'm a 98-pound weakling."

They kissed and grabbed each other, tightly. Eric's hands traveled up her back and then towards her chest. Terry drew away and said, "Hey, no more funny stuff. I've still got to get my tapes together, and we have to stop for the food."

As they walked down to the special foreigner's cafeteria, Terry and Eric held hands. They passed Comrade Li at the front desk. She glanced disapprovingly at their joined hands and nodded at them. Terry held Eric's hand tighter and smiled broadly.

"What are you doing, Miss Loo?" Eric said playfully. "I am going to be out of favor with Comrade Li, and then how will I get my extra roll of toilet paper this month?"

"Oh, I'm sure Madame Spy can accommodate you as she does every month."

Terry and Eric walked to the English Department where the dance was being held. They cleared all the desks and chairs to the side and turned off the lights. Terry lighted a few candles on the tables where the food was set, and soon the dreary classroom was transformed into a dance hall.

Eric gallantly asked each female to dance with him. At first, most of the teachers refused. But one, Miss Zhao, was a beautiful ballroom dancer and taught him a few steps. Some of Terry's foreign friends arrived from the Friendship Hotel and the Beijing Hotel, and soon there were about fifty people dancing and watching. Terry left the room to go to the bathroom. She was surprised to see so many people out in the hall and even in the other rooms, talking.

"Hello!" shouted Zhang, in a loud high-pitched tone. He had changed his shirt into a clean white one, but he still wore the same baggy blue pants he wore every day. He smiled nervously.

"Oh, hi Mr. Zhang. Why aren't you dancing?"

"I have no… no form."

"Everybody can dance. You just move."

Zhang stopped smiling and suddenly became very serious.

"Miss Loo, may I say something?"

"Sure."

He seemed very uncomfortable and was actually sweating.

"What's wrong, Mr. Zhang?"

He patted his hand back and forth above his heart. Terry was a little alarmed.

"Are you okay?"

He nodded his head and said, "Okay."

Zhang motioned to a room across the hall and they sat down at the desks.

"Miss Loo, you are kind."

Terry looked at him, quizzically. Zhang was one of her older students, a few years older than her—maybe 28, 29, with a wife in the countryside.

"Are you okay, Mr. Zhang?"

"Yes, yes. Can you keep a secret, Miss Loo?"

"Yes, of course." Terry said earnestly. It seems that everyone was always telling her secrets in this country.

"I must say..." he paused anxiously, his eyes darting towards the door and then back to Terry. "I not love my wife. I like...you."

"What?" Terry was shocked. She had no idea Zhang felt this way. "Mr. Zhang, what are you talking about? I'm your teacher."

"Yes, I know. I am mad...I hope... we be friends?"

"Of course, yes, we will be friends, but just friends... I should be getting back..."

Zhang put his head down and said, "Dui bu qi, I make trouble for you. I am sad."

"No, that's okay."

"I have to tell you true feelings. Because...I don't know what happens...we march to Square tomorrow."

Zhang sighed and suddenly grabbed her hand with his sweaty one. He looked almost mournful.

Terry didn't know what to do. She could see he was serious. Just then, someone called for her and Terry quickly released her hand from his grasp and hurried out of the room, leaving Zhang in the dark.

# ALL DAY LONG
## By Yvonne Ng


I just want to make love to you all day long.

To thread my legs through yours.
To inhale that Irish Spring soap you use.
To caress your arm with my thumb.
Writing messages, naughty lyrics
And quarter notes of love.

I want to cry out, Oh my god or
I love you while you and I reach
Ecstasy and bliss.

I want you to believe that
What we have is
Something that can
Last forever.

That you live to make me happy,
Make me dinner, draw on me.

That you know I am the most
Beautiful woman in your life –
Gorgeous in and out.

That you appreciate my roaming
Scar – badge of strength – and you can leave
A trail of bliss with your touch.

That there is nothing else you'd
Rather do than

Make love

To Me

All

Day

Long.

# DRACULINA
By Amanda Chiang

Everyone knows Dracula, the only vampire so infamous that a book was written about him. He was so infamous that every vampire, big and small, adored him. Hardly any attention was paid to his little sister, Draculina.

Draculina tried ever so hard to make friends with all the other vamplings, but it was so difficult. Perhaps her short fangs much shorter than a normal vampling's—would become longer when she grew up, but there was nothing she could do about playing in the dark. All the other vamplings got to romp about after the sun set because they would be invisible, but Draculina could be seen in the dark, and all the vamplings scorned her because she was so weird. Nobody could see her in the sun, however, which made all the vampires and vamplings very jealous of her because they couldn't become invisible in the sun. So Draculina was a very lonely vampling, having no friends to play with in the sun or in the dark.

Halloween was the toughest day of all. All the vamplings would go trick-or-treating in the cemeteries, and Draculina would have to stay in her cave. Year after year she looked longingly after their shadows, wishing with all her heart that she could go. But putting herself out at night was too dangerous— she would attract predators, and in turn endanger the whole vampire neighborhood.

It was a chilly September night, and Draculina was in her cave reading Dracula when whispers of the news reached her pointy ears:

Two vamplings had disappeared, and the elder vampires were worried a small group of predators had discovered their caves.

Draculina put down her book and inched quietly to the opening of her cave, careful to keep her whole body inside. But the elder vampires saw her anyway, and their eyes narrowed and sharpened as they glared at her.

Draculina's heart thumped and she scurried back inside. She had a very bad feeling that they thought it was her fault, that she had made herself visible and led the predators here to their home. But that was impossible. She never went out at night. Never.

A month passed, and three more vamplings disappeared. Now all accusations turned toward Draculina, and warning notes from the vampire cops piled up in her cave, ordering her to stay indoors at all times. Draculina was very sad, but there was nothing she could do to prove her innocence.

Halloween soon arrived again, but this year, there was no trick-or-treating. The Mayor announced in the evening that the event was cancelled—no one wanted to see any more vamplings disappear. All the vamplings screamed or cried or threw themselves on the ground and kicked with all their might, but the Mayor was ready for them. She handed out bags of treats to each vampling in the caves, and that quieted them down.

As the Mayor paraded through the neighborhood, a thought began to hatch in Draculina's mind. No vampling was going out this Halloween, but she would.

Draculina said goodbye to her books, her bed, and

the picture of her brother hanging on the wall. She waited until the Mayor had left, and set out.

Trembling, Draculina stepped out of her cave and made a beeline for the cemeteries to the west. She paused midway, turned her head, and there they were: three large shadows on broomsticks diving straight towards her. The predators.

Yes, she thought. They've come out. Terrified screams and shouts echoed faintly behind her.

Quickly she sped past the cemeteries, the rolling hills, and leaped down the cliff. She skimmed across the ocean, through the forest, past her brother's castle, and up the steep, stone mountain to the secret cave her brother had showed her once. Draculina desperately hoped the big boulder was still there.

She raced to the top of the mountain, and found the cave just as she remembered. The big, rectangular boulder still sat there, and Draculina crossed her fingers, praying for her plan to work.

She could almost feel the predators breathing down her back, and she dashed in the narrow opening, the predators swooping in after her. Their sharp fingers clawed into her shoulders and arms as she frantically tried to work the boulder loose, tilted sideways with a log cleverly wedged in place. Draculina kicked and pushed the log with all the strength she had, and the boulder fell in place, shutting her in with angry screeches that rang inside the stone mountain for a long, long time.

No one ever saw Draculina or the predators again, and no one ever knew what happened to them. The vampires and vamplings lived in guilty peace afterwards, and they felt even worse when a vampling confessed he had snuck out in daylight one day and that was how the predators came.

They carved a marble statue of Draculina so her story would not be forgotten, and set her in one of the cemeteries. From now on she would be able to join all the other vamplings every Halloween.

# SKY
By Cynthia Yee

I can hear the whirring of my mother's Singer sewing machine as I skip up the stairs. I enter our second floor apartment at 116 Hudson Street. I see her bent over her machine. It faces the window where she could see that dirty milk sky if she looks up but she seldom did. I look out the window to see the cars rushing by on the Southeast Expressway. I tell her about my school day, how the teacher had brown dots on her jiggly arms and heated up canned yellow soup on the radiators. I told her how the teacher wore thick high heels and a furry animal with eyes around her shoulder. She said Americans are like that. They eat canned food and they have brown dots on their skin. Not like us. We only eat fresh greens, rice, and fresh fish and meat and don't get brown dots on our skin. She never explained the animal around the American teacher's shoulder.

Sometimes my mother talks to me about her old life in China while she hangs the wash on the clothesline that reached from our window to the tree branch in the backyard. The Tree of Heaven it is called. She teaches me how to color: red goes well with green and orange with blue, my mother says. I arrange my crayons in my crayon box in that order so I would remember. I flip collars and cuffs and fold the College Town shirts in a neat pile for Norman, the factory owner, who will pick them up. We use our own machine and our own electricity. Sometimes she sends me to the factory on Edinboro Street to get spools of thread. I stand on my toes to pull the rope of the freight elevator and ride up to P&L Sportswear where Laila, Norman's wife, greets me with spools of red thread.

My mother would sew until well past midnight. I can hear the click as she turns off the machine just a few minutes before my dad returns home from the Cathay House on Beach Street where he works as a maitre d'. She times it so my father would not know how late she was working. My mother makes fifty cents a shirt and was very proud to hear when she applied for Social Security that she had earned $10,000 in her lifetime, sewing shirts facing that dirty milk sky and that Expressway which would also someday take our Chinatown home.

*Dedicated to the memory of my talented mother, May-Soon Gee Yee, for all her hard work and love for me.*

# MYSTERY IN A POT
By Pong Louie

It had been a long drive up to Ten Mile River Scout Camp in the Peekskills from Hollis. Yiu Ming Lee stumbled out of the old blue VW camper with the huge decals of a fish and the words "Striper Swiper" on the front doors. His legs felt rubbery. He rubbed his eyes, stretched and yawned as his best friend, Tony Tito followed him out. All the other groggy kids got out, except the new kid, who seemed to shrink into the corner of the back seat. He didn't move.

"What's wrong with that kid?" Yiu Ming asked as he turned to look up into Tony's round face. Yiu Ming was three months older than Tony, but a couple of inches shorter and a good ten pounds lighter, having already lost his baby fat.

"I don't know...maybe he's just shy." Tony answered.

"Hey, Ernie, come on out. We're here. Look at this huge camp and all the trees. Aren't you excited?" Yiu Ming encouraged Ernie Montalban.

"Yeah, come on, Ernie, it's time for fun. Time to hike up that mountain," Tony pointed a chubby finger into the distance.

Ernie stayed put with a confused look on his face. Mr. Ross, the scoutmaster, took Ernie's hand and led him out of the van. Ernie looked tiny next to Mr. Ross' bulk. A breeze blew and made Mr. Ross' whispy brown hair stand up and Yiu Ming wondered why all balding men's hair looked like that.

As Yiu Ming grabbed his duffle bag, he asked,

"Mr. Ross, what's wrong with Ernie?"

"Nothing really. You know that he's not a member of the troop, so he doesn't know anyone. He just came here a couple of months ago from the Philippines and his English isn't that good."

"Tony responded, "Oh, so that's it. Come on, Yiu, let's help him out."

The steep, rocky path up to their campsite was hard for Yiu Ming and Tony, but even tougher for Ernie. They tried to help him as best they could. Yiu Ming wiped the sweat off his face with his sleeves.

Fred Roman zipped by. "Why are you idiots making it hard for yourselves? Let the wimp fend for himself."

"You're the biggest kid here. Why don't you follow the scout oath for once and "help other people at all times"? Yiu Ming yelled.

"Or the scout slogan to "do a good turn daily"? Tony added.

Fred snickered and continued up the path, his muscular legs bulging, "Idiots!"

An hour later, their campsite was all set up, the big green canvas tents forming a semi-circle around the campfire circle. The tarp covered two picnic tables to one side with the black wood-burning stove and patrol box at one end.

Yiu Ming examined the patrol box as he wiped sweat off his face again, turning his sleeves black.

"Tony, this thing is cool. It opens down so you can use it as a table and all the pots and stuff fit on the shelves inside."

"Yeah, awesome," Tony said and closed the lid.

Quietly, Ernie opened the lid again, put the pot

from his mess kit on one of the shelves and closed it again.

"Hey, Ernie, what's in your pot?" Yiu Ming asked.

Ernie glanced at them and shrugged.

"What he means is that it's none of your business," Fred said.

"What do you think it is?" Tony whispered to Yiu Ming.

"How do I know. Let's take a look when he's not watching."

After lunch, Mr. Ross took the troop on a nature hike, teaching the scouts about the different trees and plants. When they got back to their campsite, everyone was tired. Mr. Ross was panting, his big round chest and belly heaving in and out. Ernie snuck a look at his pot.

Yiu Ming became more and more curious about the pot. He and Tony volunteered to cook dinner.

"Now we can see what's in that pot of his," Yiu Ming whispered to Tony. But Ernic was always watching while they cooked, taking peeks now and then.

"What do you think?" Tony asked softly.

"Dunno, it's something white; why's he keep looking in it?"

"Maybe it's crack and he's getting his hit?" Tony suggested.

They had a campfire at night and still hadn't found out what was in the pot. Before they knew it, it was taps and they had to go to sleep. In their tent, Yiu Ming said, "Let's get up early and look in that pot of his. I can't stand it, not knowing. I must have been a cat in a previous life. Curiosity is killing me.

"How early? You know I hate getting up early."

"Come on, how else we gonna find out what's in the pot? I'll wake you up."

"Man! Oh, alright. Let's get to sleep then."

"Hey, Tony, wake up," Yiu Ming said quietly, shaking Tony.

"Uuuuhhh! I wanna sleep. What time's it?"

"Seven, come on, let's see what's in the pot."

Quickly and quietly, they got dressed and emerged from their tent. Yiu Ming took a couple of steps and stopped dead. Tony ran into him.

"What the..." Tony exclaimed and peeked around Yiu Ming.

There was Ernie with his pot. Startled, he dropped it with a crashed onto the open cover, spilling its contents.

They rushed over. "Rice!" Yiu Ming exclaimed.

Tony helped Ernie get his raw rice back into the little pot, saying, "Ernie, you want rice? Why didn't you just say so? Yiu Ming can help you make it."

"Me? My mother makes it. I just eat it."

"Come on, Yiu, you can figure it out. Just help the kid."

Reluctantly, Yiu Ming went to the spigot to wash the rice. He saw a red vine with clusters of three leaves growing together, near the spigot. He thought about what he knew about poison ivy.

"Hey Tony, come here and bring a plastic bag."

"What for?"

"Just bring it here and I'll show you."

"See this? Doesn't it look like poison ivy? Use the bag and take a piece of it and put it with Fred's stuff and see what happens. I'll wash the rice and get

it going."
They high fived each other.

# ODES OF ACTIVISM

By Amanda Chiang, Gay Eng, Jackie Kim, Pong
Louie, Yvonne Ng, and Cynthia Yee


What do you do when men holding Justice are
holding her upside down? What do you do when the
semblance of fair is so crooked, twisted, and locked
up that all appears as confusion that begets rage, that
begets anger, and is gonna be gettin' you?

No time to reconsider. The course of action is
clear. Now it's about execution. The roadmap is
drawn, no snags in the road to sway from the 'x'
marking the spot. And even if there were snags,
nothing that an iron fist can't hammer through or
straight or back on the side of right. No room for
regrets but that inevitable fear – use it to keep you
warm against the cold of apathy. No movement, no
change, no change, no nothing. You'll end up where
you started so one step at a time. The footsteps are
sure because the steel tipped boots can protect you
from the splinters and the broken. Right is the side.


--


I could hear the whirring sound of my mother's
Singer sewing machine as I skipped up the stairs. I
entered our second floor apartment on Hudson Street
and I would see her bent over her machine everyday.
It faced the window where she could see that dirty
milk sky if she looked up but she didn't. I looked out
the window and I saw the cars rushing by on the
Expressway. I told her about my school day, how the

white teachers with brown dotted arms heated up canned yellow soup on the radiators. Sometimes my mother talked to me as she hung the wash on the clothesline that reached from our window to the tree branch in the backyard. The Tree of Heaven it was called. She taught me how to color: red went well with green and orange with blue, my talented seamstress mother said. I helped her flip collars and cuffs and fold the College Town shirts in a neat pile so Norman, the factory man, could pick them up. We used our own machine and our own electricity. Sometimes she would send me to the factory on Edinboro Street where I would pull the rope of the freight elevator and ride up to P&N Sportswear to pick up spools of thread. She would usually sew until well past midnight. I could hear her turn off the machine just a few minutes before my dad returned home from the Cathay House on Beach Street where he worked as a maitre di. She timed it so my father would not know how late she was working. He didn't like her to sew so late. My talented mother made fifty cents a shirt and was proud to learn from the Social Security office that she had earned $10,000 in her lifetime sewing shirts, facing that dirty milk sky and that Expressway that would also someday take our home.

--

A model of justice seized.

The Tam Brothers case started with anger. How could they arrest the victims and charge them with murder? And how could I want to be part of the legal system that allowed it to happen? People organized. A friend, a new criminal lawyer got his firm to take the case and defend the two brothers, whose family had been assigned to the public housing in Charlestown. The family had been harassed non-stop. One day, on the way home from the subway, one of the brothers was hit in the forehead with a rock. They decided to run home and avoid trouble. When they turned a corner, trouble was waiting for them. A dozen teens, "Townies", were waiting to attack them. The two brothers defended themselves the best they knew how. A Townie girl ended up dead and the brothers were charged with murder. Community people were outraged and attended the trial everyday to show their support, resulting in a happy ending. They were acquitted and exonerated. They had done nothing wrong. There was no malicious act on their part and the jury agreed. The Tam Brothers were considered innocent, except for being immigrants.

--

asian american studies

struggling
to educate
and inform
about
how
Amerika
screwed
    us:
excluded
    us,

restricted
 us,
interned
 us,
silenced
 us,
stereotyped
 us,
whitewashed
 us,
and then
pointed
to us
as
models.


--


Two sides, both right.

I love Taiwan, but having been born in the US, I felt that a little part of my root was still here. Studying abroad was the perfect opportunity, so I did all I could to get into a school, regardless of the subject I'll be studying. After a couple of years, I finally realized that what I was searching for was my childhood in the States, the life I had before I left. I was pulled out of that childhood life half reluctantly, half eagerly. Reluctant to leave, eager for what awaited me. It is affection for my childhood memories—for Cheerios, for swings, for large patches of grass, to name a few—that made me want to come back. How weird it is, to miss the States when I'm in Taiwan, and miss Taiwan when I'm in the States. I need to find a lifestyle where I can travel between both countries often, a compromise for my bicultural self: Asian and American.

--

I know the world I live in today looks a lot different from the world of decades before. We have moved forward. I have never feared that my family would have to relocate to a compound in the dusty Arizona desert, segregated from the rest of my fellow Americans. I have never felt frustrated and unempowered that the country that I call home has a web of rules that I cannot navigate or understand. I have never felt that my voice did not deserve to be heard or that what I need is unimportant. But I know it was not always this way. I know that others before me have felt that their voices were hidden behind louder voices, that their needs were not met. I know that others before me felt betrayed by the country they adopted as their home, separated and unaccepted, unwelcome and unheard. I know what it feels like to be different, but I know I have a debt to those that came before me.

--

Immigrant poetry

I will always be an immigrant
New to the land,
Just as my mother
and great great grandfather were.
Fresh faced and scared,

Daring and struggling
Adapting to this land.

It's a story of vectoral displacement,
Tears and good-byes,
Hope and revelation
This land that brings
Upward mobility and downward despair.
We have our two-story house on Briar Patch Drive,
But do the neighbors let us in?
--

*This ode was written to celebrate the 30th anniversary of the Asian American Resource Workshop and was performed by members of the Writers' Group at the 2009 banquet.*

# ABOUT THE AUTHORS

## Alison Chan

Alison Chan currently divides her time between Boston and the Antipodes. Though she once worked as an Emergency Room physician, her passion is literature. For the last five years, she has attempted to write poems, short stories, and various drafts of novels.

It's extremely dangerous to let her visit a bookstore or Amazon.com. She owns no pets, but loves honeybees, ducks, Australian parrots, and dolphins.

## Amanda Chiang

If you see a girl with her nose in a book and munching on Cheerios, that's me.

If you see a girl sitting on a beach and staring far off into the horizon, that's me.

An aspiring writer who loves to read, daydream, and travel.

## Gay Eng

Gay Eng grew up in a laundry in Upstate New York. She's travelled the world seeking and creating stories and poems. She's been writing forever and ever, and hopes to never stop.

## Pong Louie

Pong Louie grew up in New York City, where he was born. Having inherited the love of writing from his father, Louis Chu, Pong has been writing since he was in elementary school. The wise-guy in him often shows through in his writing, whether he's writing about the Asian-American experience, a mystery or something else.

## Yvonne Ng

Yvonne Ng is a native Bostonian and fell in love with words at a very young age. She's inspired by the talented members of the AARW Writers' Group and is grateful to share, learn, and tell stories.

## Cynthia Yee

*Cynthia Yee at the Grand Canyon, Arizona*

Cynthia Yee is an educator, writer, storyteller, and dabbler. She was born and raised in Boston's Chinatown. She has taught in Chinatown and in Brookline, Massachusetts and trained many student teachers. She is the Co-founder and Facilitator of the Asian-American Resource Workshop Writers' Group. This supportive group has evolved to become an international group connected through modern technology and friendship. She enjoys Art classes and other creative activities, and is an avid traveler and walker. She likes to savor good food and movies of all types. Ethnic and open air markets, cafes, museums, good books and nature hikes are favorite sources of inspiration. She relishes the grandeur and beauty of the National Parks for entertaining broader perspectives. She loves Cape Cod. When she floats in the Atlantic looking up at the blue sky she feels like she is in paradise.

## Karen S. Young

Karen is a taiko drummer who was hoping that she would learn some writing skills through occasionally hanging out with other writers.